"I've come b
marry you...

Mattie froze in pl

She couldn't look Samuel full in the face. It was too painful. He might have a few differences from her David, but in the right light, she was sure even their mother couldn't tell them apart. All except for that scar. "What?"

"I promised David—" Samuel swallowed hard "—that if anything were to happen to him, I would take care of his wife...his family."

"Take care of?"

"Marry."

"No." The word shot from her mouth. "No," she said again.

"I told him—"

"No." She shook her head as she began to pace.

This wasn't happening. But it was. This couldn't be real, but the air was cool on her heated cheeks. The smell of someone's early fire drifted to her on the breeze. There was no denying it.

She whirled around to face Samuel Byler, the stranger with a familiar face. Yet was he a stranger?

There had been a time when she'd thought she knew him well enough...but that was a long time ago.

Born and bred in Mississippi, **Amy Lillard** is a transplanted Southern belle who now lives in Oklahoma with her deputy husband and two spoiled cats. When she's not creating happy endings, she's an avid football fan (go Chiefs!), an adoring mother to an almost-adult son and loves binge-watching television shows. Amy is an award-winning author with more than sixty novels and novellas in print. She loves to hear from readers. You can find her on Facebook, Instagram, Twitter, Goodreads, TikTok and Pinterest. You can email her at amylillard@hotmail.com or check out her website, amywritesromance.com.

Books by Amy Lillard

Love Inspired

The Amish Christmas Promise

Visit the Author Profile page at LoveInspired.com.

The Amish
Christmas Promise

Amy Lillard

LOVE INSPIRED
INSPIRATIONAL ROMANCE

LOVE INSPIRED®
INSPIRATIONAL ROMANCE

ISBN-13: 978-1-335-59847-9

The Amish Christmas Promise

Copyright © 2023 by Amy Lillard

For questions and comments about the quality of this book, please contact us at CustomerService@Harlequin.com.

Love Inspired
22 Adelaide St. West, 41st Floor
Toronto, Ontario M5H 4E3, Canada
www.LoveInspired.com

Printed in U.S.A.

Now faith is the substance of things hoped for, the evidence of things not seen.
—*Hebrews* 11:1

To Rob. Always.

Acknowledgments

This book is a dream come true for me.
I have always wanted to write for Harlequin.
Though it was a long time in the making,
here we are! First let me thank my agent,
Nicole Resciniti, and everyone at the
Seymour Agency for helping me make my
dream a reality. Thank you to my editor,
Johanna Raisanen, and the Love Inspired team
for making this book the best it could be.
And a special thanks to my husband, Rob,
aka The Major. You make everything a dream
come true!

I know there are probably a million other
people who deserve a shout-out, but as usual,
it's impossible to name them all. You know
who you are. Thank you for being there.

And a special thanks to all the readers
who make writing possible. You are the best!

Chapter One

Samuel Byler paid the driver, then looked down the narrow lane that lay before him as the man drove away. He should have felt something more. Something more than a sense of relief. A stab of longing maybe? He was home. Something he hadn't been able to say for many years now. Yet, not really home, but back in the valley where he had grown up.

He started up the drive toward the house he couldn't yet see. His brother's house. Used to be, anyway. Now it belonged to David's widow, Mattie. If the location app the driver used was correct, it wasn't far off the road, just behind a copse of trees. It was behind one of those trees where he left his duffel bag. He didn't want to show up at Mattie's house toting everything he owned like a vagabond.

A tingle started in his back and worked its

way up to his neck. His clothes felt too tight, unfamiliar. They should have been like donning the past. That was what he was doing, wasn't it? Going back. Back but not backward. He had to remember that.

As the house came into view, he stopped, finally hit by a wave of nostalgia. Returning to Kishacoquillas Valley after so long... Not even just the valley, but to the tiny community of Millers Creek nestled there. He may have only been in western Pennsylvania, but he had been a world away from home.

But this house was new. Built only a handful of years ago. Like most in the area, it barely had a porch to speak of. Off to one side was a small barn, painted red and open, as if the morning chores had already been completed. On the other side of that was a long building just like the one he had seen in the newspaper article. The milking barn. For goats. That had to have been her idea, his brother's wife. David was a model son, but Samuel couldn't imagine him willingly choosing to milk goats every day of his life. Not even after four years in prison.

Samuel sucked in a calming breath and pushed his resentment down deep inside. It was a fluke, really, maybe a miracle that he had seen the article at all. About the tragic accident that had taken his brother's life. If he hadn't run across it, would his family have even let him know that his twin was dead? He knew the answer and hated it even though he understood that was their way. He was dead to them all, and the dead can't be notified.

An old yellow dog ambled out to meet him. The beast came at him half-hearted as if she knew it was what she was supposed to do, but she was unable to muster any enthusiasm for the chore.

She barked with each step she took, the sound somewhat menacing, though no teeth bared. It seemed the pooch didn't want a confrontation almost as much as he himself didn't.

Samuel squatted and reached out a hand toward the dog, only then realizing the truth.

"Goldie?"

The dog stopped barking and wagged her tail, the motion nearly knocking her over as she tried to come near.

"Aw, Goldie. When did you get so old?"

When had any of them gotten so old? But whereas the age was beginning to show on his face at the corners of his eyes and mouth, on the dog it came in the gray hair around her muzzle and the watery look in her eyes. He could see it in her physical motions as well. She used to run and bound and play, but that had been a lifetime ago. Eight years or better. He should have known that David would have brought her with him when he married. He just never expected her to still be around.

Samuel gave Goldie one final scratch behind the ear, then stood and looked around. David had done well enough for himself. A house on the edge of their father's property. Of course. Because David had been the good brother, the one who stayed, helped farm the family land, took care of their father in his final days, supported their mother, got married…did everything right.

He blew out a harsh breath. What was he doing there?

It wasn't a question he could ask himself. He was there because of a promise and it was a promise that he would keep. But how could he measure up? How could he step into his brother's shoes? Especially when David had been the good brother and he had been the rogue. Everyone said so. He had broken his mother's heart too many times to count, from his wild *rumspringa* to his packing up and leaving for the other side of the state. Still, his mother had always forgiven him, even when he was sure she wouldn't. Even in those times when he was certain she had her doubts, she had always forgiven him, just like the Lord. Then his father had stepped in and declared him dead to the family. Samuel hadn't been back since.

But he was changed now. The love of a good woman would do that for a man, even when religion and family failed. He wasn't the same person he had been when he left. Not the same at all.

Changed but still unworthy. And yet here he stood.

"No time like the present, Byler," he muttered to himself and started toward the house. Two stairs and he was staring at the door. He raised his hand to knock, but it was jerked open before his knuckles met wood.

"What do you want?" the woman demanded. She had brown hair and was a petite thing. It was hard to tell as she was stooped at the waist, her forearms braced on aluminum crutches. Mattie's sister Evie. He recognized her immediately. She hadn't changed all that much over the years. Like everyone, just grown a little older.

"I—"

"What do you want?" She moved her crutches into a wider stance. He thought perhaps to seem more forceful, then he heard a small bleat. A tiny goat stood next to her. She was white with black stockings on each leg and a small smudge under her nose. Samuel couldn't decide if it was a kid or a pygmy.

"I'm here to see M—" He didn't get her name out before a loud clatter interrupted. He peered inside and followed the noise.

She was standing by the long dining table, her chair sprawled out behind her as if she had stood up in such haste that she had knocked it over.

Her shock was expected. He supposed, to her, he looked like her husband come back from the dead.

"Mattie," Evie called. She didn't wait for her sister to respond. With a surprising agility, she whipped around, her crutches clanking as she did so. Somehow, she managed to push the goat to one side and haul herself toward her sister.

Mattie's face had turned chalk white, her eyes a little dazed. She placed one hand over the mound of her pregnant belly, then slowly crumpled like a marionette's puppet whose strings had been cut.

Samuel pushed over the threshold, side-stepped the little goat and managed to catch Mattie before she hit the floor. She had grabbed ahold of the edge of the table to stop her descent.

He held her with one hand while bending down to set her chair back right. Behind him, the goat bleated once more.

"Be quiet, Charlie," Evie admonished.

Samuel continued to support Mattie as she

slowly lowered herself into the seat. He squatted down next to her.

He could only imagine what it was like for her to see his face, nearly identical to her husband's. The husband she had just buried a few months ago. He felt for her in that regard, though he could no more control what his face looked like than he could the weather.

"I'm sorry," he said.

Evie scoffed, but he paid her no mind. There would be more than the likes of her who objected to his plans, his return, his past; he couldn't let the opinion of one scrap of a woman set his feet on a different course. A promise was a promise.

"Who was outside?" a different woman asked.

He could see her out of the corner of his eye, standing at the base of the stairs. Another sister he was certain, though he couldn't tell which one. Eight years was a long time.

"Come see for yourself, Naomi," Evie answered. Naomi. Yes, another sister. Twin to Priscilla, if he was remembering correctly. Though the two of them were not identical as he and David were.

For a moment he wondered how many other Ebersol girls were stashed about. There were a lot of them, he recalled. Five or six, to be certain.

"Samuel," Naomi sputtered.

"Are you okay?" He kept his eyes on the woman in front of him. She had hers closed, her breathing shallow, and her face still devoid of color.

She nodded, though she didn't open her eyes. The goat made her way to Mattie's side, pushing her nose under Mattie's hand as if demanding attention. She bushed her fingers across the goat's tiny head as if in a dream.

"I think you should go," Evie said.

"Why did you even let him in?" Naomi demanded.

"I didn't let him in. He just barged past me."

"Are you going to faint?" he asked Mattie. "Put your head between your knees."

She scoffed and let out a bitter laugh. "That's not going to happen." Then she pushed his hand away from the back of her neck. Until then he hadn't realized that he was touching her.

"You shouldn't be here," Naomi said. She moved closer to the table where her sister sat. Where he still crouched next to her.

Charlie the goat danced to one side to avoid her approach.

She was right. He shouldn't be there. He was not right with the church. They could get in trouble for just talking to him. That was something he had to rectify first off. Well, after this. This was the most important.

"I didn't mean to scare you," he said.

"You didn't." This time she did look at him but only for a brief moment. Her eyes ricocheted off him like a BB against metal.

Scared might not be the best word, but he had taken her completely by surprise. He didn't need her confirmation to know that. No one knew that he had plans of returning. Not even his own family. He wasn't ready for that confrontation. He had enough to work out with Mattie without adding the rest of his family into the mix.

"I came to talk to you. Are you okay with that?"

"No!" both sisters hollered at the same time.

Mattie nodded slowly, as if she was reluctant to agree. Maybe that was a good sign.

It was then that the sweet scent of pancakes permeated his system. He had been so focused on the task he needed to complete that he hadn't noticed what was right in front of him.

A large stack of pancakes sat in the middle of the table along with a butter dish and a bottle of maple syrup. The table itself had been set for three.

Charlie had moved around to the other side and was determinedly head-butting one of the chairs as if to push it away so she could climb up. With what he knew about goats—which truly wasn't a lot—he figured that she was trying to secure her own place for the meal.

"You were about to eat breakfast."

"Jah," Mattie whispered.

"You really should go." Naomi cast a quick glance at Evie, then took a step forward as if she was going to physically remove him from the house if he didn't willingly leave.

"I just want to talk to you," he said quietly, his attention fixed on his brother's widow.

She shook her head, but once again, the action seemed almost hesitant.

"He was my brother."

"No one's disputing that," Evie said.

"The bishop—" Naomi started.

"The bishop doesn't know I'm here. No one does. Just the four of us."

"I—" Mattie started. Then she closed her eyes and sat quietly for a moment.

She knows.

The thought was ridiculous. Yet was it? What if David had told her of their plans? Why would he? How was David supposed to know when he was going to die? He hadn't. Just like he hadn't on that long-ago day when he made Samuel promise.

In all fairness, David had promised too, but it hadn't come down to him keeping his own. Just the one Samuel had made to his twin.

"I need to eat something," she finally said.

"I can wait in the barn."

"Outside," Naomi corrected. "On the porch."

"It's chilly out today," Mattie said. "It's supposed to rain."

"*Jah.* It is," he murmured in return. The sky was heavy with gray clouds, a sure sign that winter was on its way.

"You can wait in the living room," Mattie finally said.

"What?" Evie screeched while at the same time Naomi cried out, "No!"

"You can wait in the living room while we eat, then we can talk. You can say whatever it is that you came to say."

She didn't need to voice the rest in order for him to hear it. *Then you have to leave.*

But that wasn't the plan. Not by a long shot.

That was a bridge he would only be able to cross when he got to it.

"Thank you," he said. He stood and removed his hat.

The two women glared at him as he made his way to the large tan-colored couch sitting to one side of the fireplace.

The sisters moved toward Mattie. Their posture was protective as if she needed to be saved from him.

Charlie the goat had managed to push the

chair back and had just climbed into it, her intention to steal breakfast clear.

He settled down onto the sofa and tried to make himself as inconspicuous as possible.

"Get down, you rotten beast," Naomi said, though her voice held a note of affection.

Chairs scraped across the linoleum floor as they each took their place at the table.

Samuel propped his hat on his knee, then moved it to the cushion next to him. He didn't know what to do with his hands, so he stacked them one on top of the other in his lap. Then he reversed them. He hadn't been this nervous the first time he had taken Viola King home from a singing. But that had been a lifetime ago. Another life entirely.

The girls bowed their heads for the silent prayer.

How long had it been since he had seen anyone pray, to themselves or otherwise? He shifted in his seat and stared into the empty fireplace. It wouldn't be long until cold weather set in and a fire would be blazing in order to keep warm. He had missed having a fire in the wintertime. He couldn't say he missed chopping wood, but it was a chore that was worth it in the end.

He repositioned his hands once more, then felt a cold nudge and a small nibble. "Hi," he whispered to the goat. She was really a cute thing.

But he could tell right off that she was as mischievous as they come, probably a little spoiled as a house pet and very loved by the women.

Charlie bleated in response, then hopped onto the couch next to him. She settled down there as if the place had been made just for her. She rested her chin on his leg.

He petted her head. At least now he had something to do with his hands.

"Here."

He jerked his attention upward as Mattie thrust a plate toward him.

It was piled high with pancakes smothered in butter and maple syrup. A small pile of bacon sat to the side, soaking up the overpour of sweetness. A fork rested opposite. His stomach growled just looking at the food. He hadn't eaten anything before heading out this morning. He had been too nervous.

"Take it," she said, pushing it toward him once again.

Not knowing what else to do, he accepted the plate.

"You can't eat at the table, but David would be disheartened to know that you were here and I didn't offer you something, shunned or not." Her gaze didn't meet his.

"Thank you," Samuel said.

She gave a small nod. "And don't give Charlie too many bites of the pancakes. The syrup gives her gas."

Before he could ask how many was too many, she turned and went back to her place at the table.

He could feel their gazes on him as he ate. Not Mattie's, but the other two. They were watching him like a mouse keeps an eye on a hawk, wary and untrusting. He couldn't blame them for that. He hadn't given anyone in the district reason to trust him, but that was about to change.

They finished the meal in silence. Samuel had a feeling that if he hadn't been there, they would have been as chatty as magpies, going on about the goats David and Mattie had decided to raise, material for dresses and maybe even things for the baby. But he also knew that Amish women were careful about what they did in advance of actually having a baby. It wasn't right to become too arrogant and expect a healthy delivery. That was something to pray for, but not take for granted.

When they finished, they stood, forgoing the second prayer after the meal. He supposed it was becoming a lost ritual.

Mattie made her way over to him.

He had finished as well and was holding the plate in the air out of the goat's reach. When

Mattie approached, he gently pushed Charlie from his lap and stood, offering his reluctant hostess his empty plate. "It was delicious. Thank you," he said. *"Danki."* He needed to get used to using Pennsylvania Dutch now that he was home. It would be expected of him. But after so many years, the words were rusty and strange on his tongue.

"What do you want to talk about?" she bluntly asked.

He cast a quick glance toward her sisters. Both women were standing by the table, acting like they were cleaning up, but intently watching them all the same.

"Not here." He didn't want her sisters as witnesses. Not when he felt as nervous as a long-tailed cat in a room full of rocking chairs. "On the porch?"

Once again Mattie looked as if she might decline, then she gave him one stiff nod and made her way to the front door. She grabbed a shawl off the back of a nearby rocker and wrapped it around herself.

Winter would be full on them soon. She needed his help. And he needed her to say yes. He owed his brother that much.

She opened the door and held the goat back with one foot, blocking her path as she waited for him to don his hat and follow behind her.

It felt strange to be dressed Plain again, but he supposed he would get used to it. He had no choice in the matter.

She closed the door behind them, making sure the house pet stayed inside, then she crossed her arms. Her gaze settled on his cheek. It was the closest she had come to actually looking at him. But her attention was centered just below his left eye. Samuel had a scar there. One difference between him and David. Samuel had fallen out of the tire swing they'd had as boys and cut himself on a sharp rock. It had taken seven stitches to close it up and their mother had joked that now people would be able to tell them apart. Maybe that was why Mattie was staring at it, her gaze as strong as a touch, like she was clutching at a lifeline.

"For a man who wants to talk, you certainly don't say very much."

"All right." He cleared his throat, then gathered his courage and the words he needed. There really wasn't a right way to say what needed to be said, so he blurted it out. "I've come home to marry you."

Chapter Two

Mattie froze in place. Her ears started ringing, and she was certain none of her limbs would work. Thankfully, there was a bench directly behind her. She collapsed onto it and stared at this man.

"…promised David," he was saying.

She stirred herself out of the stupor and focused on him once more. She couldn't look him full in the face. It was too painful. He might have a few differences than her David, but in the right light, she was sure even their mother couldn't tell them apart. All except for that scar. "Wh-what?" she finally managed to sputter.

"I promised David," he repeated.

Mattie shook her head and pushed back to her feet. "I heard that part. What did you promise David?"

Samuel swallowed hard. "That if anything

were to happen to him, I would take care of his wife…his family."

"Take care of?" She asked the question, but she wasn't quite sure she wanted an answer.

"Marry."

"No." The one word shot from her mouth like a slug from a rifle. "No," she said again, this time with a little less urgency, but no less force.

"I told him—"

"No." She shook her head as she began to pace.

This wasn't happening. But it was. This couldn't be real, but the air was cool on her heated cheeks. The smell of someone's early fire drifted to her on the breeze. The sky was blue; the land was brown. There was no denying it.

She whirled around to face Samuel Byler, the stranger with a familiar face. Yet was he a stranger? There had been a time when she had thought she knew him well enough, but that was a long time ago. A lot of changes in eight years.

He had moved behind her, coming after her, so close now she could smell the detergent on his clothes along with the crisp scent of the fall day.

"It's too soon," she said.

He gave a small nod, then pulled his black felt hat from his head and twirled it between his fingers. "I know. But with the…baby." He hesitated slightly before saying that last word. Pregnancy and birth weren't subjects that were talked about in mixed company. "It doesn't leave us a lot of time."

"For what?"

"To get married."

She just had to have him say those words again. "It doesn't matter what kind of time we have or don't have, because I am not marrying you. You—" She searched for a good reason that she wouldn't be able to marry him. Aside from the fact that she had only buried her husband less than a handful of months before, and she didn't really know this man offering to be her next groom. "You don't even live here."

He placed his hat back on his head. She couldn't help but notice that he cocked it a little to one side, just as David had. "I'm moving back."

"David—"

"Was a great man. Far greater than I will ever be," Samuel said. "And that's all the more reason for me to keep my promise."

"When did you make these promises?" And why hadn't David told her about them?

"After *rumspringa*. We were going through our baptism classes and—well, that was the summer when…" He paused, shook his head. "That's when Albert King died."

She remembered it well. They had all been swimming in the creek down behind the bishop's house. Everyone had been having a wonderful time. The next thing they knew, Albert was floating facedown. No one could say exactly what had happened, only that he had drowned. It had been a terrible time for them all. The whole community had been devastated, but none more than Myra Byler, David and Samuel's cousin. Myra had yet to marry another.

"We decided then and there that if something happened to one of us, then the other would take care of his family." He said the words as if they were the simplest and most natural way to behave.

"What would you have done if you had been married yourself? I assume you're not married." She waved a vague hand in the general direction of his beardless face.

"Set you up in a *dawdihaus*?" He chuckled awkwardly. "I don't know. We would have worked something out."

"But since you're not married, then I should just jump up and marry you now."

"There's more at stake than that, and you know it."

She laid a protective hand over the mound where the child rested. "We'll be fine," she said with more confidence than she actually felt. "It's God's will. He will see us through." She had to believe.

"So you're going to milk the goats twice a day, make the cheese and whatever else it is you do here and see to all the animals? Will that be before or after you cook, clean, do the laundry and make sure the baby has everything they need?"

She was not going to be put off. She would survive. She had to. She had no choice. She had sisters to help her. She was going to have another baby. In just a few months she would have three children and her husband was gone. There was nothing in the world, not even marrying Samuel Byler, that would change that.

"We can take this slowly," he continued. "Court a little. That sort of thing."

Court? She was in mourning. And pregnant. She couldn't court anyone right now. She didn't want to.

Unshed tears stung her eyes. She blinked them away. "I—"

He shook his head. "Listen. I know what you and David shared, your love for each other. It was special. I'm not trying to take his place."

"What do you call it then?" She propped her hands on her hips and told herself to stand her ground.

"Okay, maybe I am, but not in that way." He flashed her a charming smile, so much like David's it brought to mind a better time and place. But she fought against the memories.

Just what way was he talking about? Husband? Best friend? Father? Lover? The very thought made her stomach lurch.

"*Danki*, Samuel Byler. Your offer is most gracious, but I'm afraid I must decline. Good day." She spun on her heel and before he had a chance to move, she zipped into the house and closed the door behind her.

Samuel stood on the porch and merely stared at the door. What else could he do? It was painted smooth creamy white. Toward the bottom there were a few dings and smudges where someone had nudged it open with their foot on more than one occasion.

She had turned him down. Flat. Without even one hesitation. Now what was he supposed to do?

Leave her alone was one answer, but how could he do that? She thought she knew what she was getting in to, but she didn't. Even if Mattie had an easy birth, there would be no time for recovery. Livestock had to be fed every day, no matter what. No matter that a baby had just arrived. Sure, the community would rally around her and help her in her time of greatest need, but what she didn't understand was that her time for need was only beginning. A family needed a mother and a father to care and support and love a child. With his brother gone, who would love and support Mattie and her little one?

She loved David, and Samuel knew that it was going to be difficult for her to move on. But she would. Plus, Samuel was going to be there. That much he knew. One hundred percent.

After one last look at the house, he turned and made his way off the porch and down to the road. He had some planning to do.

Mattie closed the door behind her and pressed her back against it. She sucked in a deep breath, not knowing whether to laugh or cry.

"What?"

She jerked her attention to Evie. Arms braced on her crutches, her sister stood in the open doorway that led to the narrow staircase. Mattie shook her head. "I, uh—"

"Did something happen?" Naomi appeared behind Evie, so quick and close that she almost toppled her over.

"Naomi!" Evie protested.

"Sorry, it's just—"

"Are they still sleeping?" she asked.

Naomi nodded. "Must have been a bad night."

Their little family had had more than their share of bad nights since David had died. At three and half, Bethann didn't quite understand that her father was never coming back. Gracie was only eighteen months old, but still she knew that something was wrong. Both girls had taken to waking up in the night, sometimes from nightmares, sometimes for reasons that Mattie couldn't determine. But neither had slept through the night since the funeral. The lack of rest was beginning to wear on Mattie, even with her sisters there to help.

"I don't want to let them sleep too long," she murmured though she felt as if she could use a nap herself. Like she had time for that.

"Give them another half hour," Naomi suggested. "And you can tell us what happened."

"He asked me to marry him."

"What!" Evie screeched the word at a volume Mattie was certain sent half the dogs in the county to howling.

"Don't wake the girls," she admonished in a half whisper.

"I told you." Naomi pointed at Evie with a self-satisfied smile.

"You told her?" Mattie asked.

Naomi gave her a small shrug as if the idea was no big thing at all. "I had a feeling."

She had a feeling.

"You told him no, right," Evie pressed. "That's what I want to know."

Mattie stayed in place for a moment more, listening for any sound coming from the front porch. There was none; he was gone. All was quiet from the upstairs as well. She pushed herself off the door, shed her shawl and moved to the couch.

"Mattie?" Her sisters were not about to let this go.

"He asked you to marry him and then what happened?" Naomi urged.

"Actually, he didn't really ask me to marry him," she corrected absently.

"Stop talking in riddles," Evie commanded. "What happened out there?"

"He told me that he had come back to Millers Creek to marry me."

"And you said…" Naomi urged.

"I told him no." She spoke the words softly, but they sounded like the roar of a train.

"I told you," Evie said with a pointed nod in Naomi's direction.

Mattie was reeling too much from the actual proposal, if she could even call it that, to pay her sister's predictions much mind. "I can't marry him." She had just buried the only man she had ever loved. How could she remarry anyone, but especially his brother? His identical twin.

"Of course you can't," Evie said, her voice soft and supportive.

Naomi moved with lightning speed. She was seated next to Mattie in a heartbeat, while Evie came slower and sat in the chair next to them. David's chair. Not willing to be left out, Charlie jumped up next to Mattie and settled down in what was left of her lap. She mindlessly rubbed one of the goat's ears between her fingers.

"Mattie." Naomi took Mattie's hand and held it between both of her own, stilling the caress. "Maybe you should think about this."

"Naomi." Evie's tone held a beat of warning.

"What?" Naomi almost dared Evie to continue. Mattie had no idea what had been transpiring between her sisters, and truthfully, she wasn't sure she wanted to know.

"I can't marry him." Mattie stared down at the mischievous goat. She had brought her home from an auction that she and David had gone to just before his accident. The tiny beast was a handful to be sure, but with David's help, she knew Charlie would grow into a good pet for her girls. But now David was gone. Her daughters were miserable, and Charlie even more rambunctious.

Her gaze might have been centered on her

goat and her thoughts on the life that she would never have, but she saw Naomi and Evie share a look.

"Evie and I were talking earlier." Naomi sighed. "This farm is part of David's father's farm."

Mattie nodded. "It belonged to his grandfather and his great-grandfather before that."

"How are you going to keep up the farm by yourself?" Naomi asked. She didn't say it, but they all knew that Evie had promised to stay and help with the baby. Yet with her limited mobility that help was cut in half. Then add in a preschooler and a toddler and a naughty goat and it seemed a recipe for disaster. Or at the very least failure.

"I'll hire somebody." Mattie stiffened her spine but it only made her back ache.

"Who are you going to hire?" Naomi pressed.

"When the time comes, I'll think of something."

"And the baby?" Naomi asked.

"Naomi." Evie's warning sounded again.

Mattie looked at each of her sisters in turn. "I was hoping you might be able to help. And Priscilla." She was Naomi's twin. Actually, Mattie had five sisters who could lend a hand from time to time. They could all share the responsibility so no one burned out from the strain.

Evie took a deep breath and Mattie braced herself for what was to come. "You know we would do anything for you."

"Anything at all," Naomi broke in. "But waiting until the time comes is not the way to handle this. You know the Bylers will want to keep the farm in the family. You can't sell."

"I couldn't sell the farm anyway," Mattie said. She and David had worked too hard to build the place. Not the house or the regular barn, but the milking parlor, the pen for the goats and the actual farm store, which was a storage building converted with propane-run coolers to keep the products fresh. Then there was the business itself. She had gone through a lot of red tape and trouble to get the farm certified organic and to get permission to sell raw goat's milk and cheese there on the premises. Too much work to let it slip away now. She owed it to David to keep it going.

"I don't suppose all of you could move back in with *Dat*," Naomi said.

"No." That was the last thing Mattie wanted to do. She was determined to keep her farm.

"Or if you were to marry Samuel…"

Naomi didn't have to finish; Mattie knew what she was implying. If she were to marry Samuel, the farm would remain in the family— well, it would as long as he made himself right with the church—then she wouldn't lose her home, and she would have the help she needed, with the goats as well as her children.

But could she really marry Samuel? Regardless of the fact that his face lived in her memories, she didn't know him. She hadn't seen him in years. And then there was the whole problem with him and the church. Amish talked and everyone in the valley knew that once Samuel had moved away, he hadn't petitioned for a move of membership. He had simply turned away from his religion. Or at least it appeared that way. No one knew from there how he had been living. But if he came back, if he bent his knee, then the church would welcome him home. It sounded simple, but it was more complicated than words let on.

"I don't know." Mattie shook her head. Her husband had only been gone a few months. It seemed like she had just buried him. How could she possibly be thinking about getting married again? She couldn't. That was all there was to it.

Evie stood, and instinctively Mattie scooted over so she could sit on the other side of her. "You know we only want what's best for you," she said. "And little Evie." She reached out a hand and gently patted Mattie's belly.

"Don't you mean baby Naomi?" Naomi placed her own hand next to Evie's.

"Are you trying to taunt me with the thought of another girl?"

"Maybe you should have named the other two after us and you wouldn't be having to listen to this now." Naomi shot her a playfully pointed look.

"Uh-huh." But she had named both girls in honor of her mother, Anna Grace.

"Just sayin'," Evie continued, picking up the argument.

Mattie couldn't help but smile. Maybe the first one she'd had in days. "You two are really going to be shocked when it comes out a boy."

"*Mamm*, man outside." Bethann pulled on the edge of Mattie's apron to gain her attention.

Last night had been a better night all around, but only because she let both girls sleep with her. That was when she realized that they feared losing her as well. As if nighttime wasn't scary enough when you were little.

"What?" Mattie asked. She had thought Bethann had said—

"Man," she repeated. "Outside."

Mattie didn't have time to respond as Naomi called from downstairs.

"Mattie. He's here."

She didn't have to ask who Evie was talking about. Only one man could be outside. Mattie pulled in a deep breath. She needed her head about her. She didn't need to rush down there. She didn't need to fly off the handle and rant and rave that she had told him to leave the day before and she had meant leave and don't come back. She needed to be calm and levelheaded. Only that would make him see that she was serious.

"I'll be down in a minute," she called in return.

It had taken everything that she had to get out of bed that morning. The girls may have had an easier night, but for Mattie it was the daytime that strained her. So much energy to put on her black dress and comb out her hair. So much effort to go about each day. She knew it would get easier and she had to keep going. For herself. For the baby. For her girls. It was just so hard.

She gently tugged on the sides of her prayer covering and reached for her container of straight pins.

"Dat," Bethann said.

The small plastic box fell to the floor, its contents scattering.

Naomi was up the stairs in a heartbeat. "What happened?"

"I spilled my pins." She lifted Bethann into her arms to keep her from stepping on the sharp metal objects.

"You shouldn't be picking her up like that," Naomi admonished.

"You would rather I let her stab her feet?"

Bethann hated shoes. Last winter had been a struggle to keep her in footwear of any kind. But last year she had had David's help. It might be getting cooler outside, but right now, Mattie wasn't up for the battle.

"That's not what I mean and you know it. Give her to me." Naomi reached toward her niece. Bethann went easily to her.

Mattie started to bend down and gather up the spilled pins.

Naomi scoffed. "Never mind. You take her. I'll pick up this mess."

"Then I'll take care of Samuel."

"Dat," Bethann said again.

"Not *Dat*," Mattie corrected, a large lump nearly blocking the words. Just another reason why he couldn't hang around. It would confuse her daughters beyond what anyone should have to deal with.

Truthfully, he had a lot of nerve coming here, and after she told him that he couldn't court her. He might have promised David that he would take care of her, but she had no obligation to receive any help. That was on him.

"Good morning, Mattie," Evie said from her place next to the stove. She was adding cheese to their scrambled eggs. "Breakfast is just about—"

"In a minute, Evie." She quickly settled Bethann on her booster seat at the table across from Gracie, who was already in her high chair happily gnawing on a pancake while eating applesauce with her fingers.

Gracie, it seemed, hated flatware as much as her sister detested wearing shoes. Who knew what quirks the new baby would bring into their lives. Mattie didn't even want to hazard a guess.

Instead, she sidestepped Charlie and headed for the door. "Will you get Bethann her breakfast while I go—" She jerked a thumb toward the front door.

"*Jah*, of course." Evie frowned.

"What is it?"

"Nothing."

But Mattie could tell that Evie was hiding something. She wanted to tell her to spit it out already. Then again, she wasn't sure she wanted to hear it. She didn't want to hear the argument of don't marry him but allow him to work around the farm if that's what he wants to do. The idea didn't set well with her at all. If she was going to make a play as an independent businesswoman, she needed to get on with it.

She wanted him gone five minutes ago.

She went out the front door and down the

porch steps, determined to give him a piece of her mind. But he was…nowhere.

She looked around the yard, but didn't spy his familiar and strange figure. Then her gaze landed on the open barn door.

That was where he had to be. And he had to have come up on foot unless he was storing a horse in one of the stalls. A horse but no buggy. Highly unlikely.

She marched into the barn, revving herself back up for the argument that was sure to come. She really didn't have the energy for this today. Why couldn't he have taken the not-at-all-subtle hint yesterday and not come back?

"Stop what you are doing this instant," she cried before she even looked to see what he was doing. Whatever it was, she wanted him to stop.

"Good morning, Mattie. Yes, it is a lovely day. Not too cool. Not yet anyway. I heard there was a cold front coming in tonight." He was standing at the opening for the first stall, shovel in gloved hands, obviously preparing to muck it out. Her carriage mare had been moved to the small paddock just outside the open Dutch doors on the far side of the barn. He had the audacity to smile at her.

Her annoyance geared up a notch. "I mean it. I am not going to let you court me."

He raised one arm in the air, the other supporting the shovel handle. "I'm not here to court you."

Those coolly spoken words set her back a step. "You're not?"

He smiled, that stupid, charming smile once again. "I'm going to help with a few chores, then I'll be out of your way."

"Chores?" *What kind of chores?*

"Mucking out the horse stalls, checking the shoes on the Belgians. And I noticed the wagon has a few loose slats yesterday."

"My wagon?" She hadn't seen anything of the sort. But then she had been a little caught up in more important matters.

"Once I take care of those things, I'll head home."

"Oh." That effectively stopped all her arguments. "Well, that's fine. I guess you can do that." She started back to the house, then whirled on him once again. "And just because I'm letting you help a bit, don't start thinking I'm going to change my mind about courting."

The corners of his mouth twitched. "I wouldn't dream of it."

Chapter Three

Samuel watched her stomp back to the house, the strings of her prayer *kapp* streaming out behind her.

She had some spunk; he'd give her that much. But she also had way too much pride.

Pride goeth before destruction.

He knew that all too well. Just as he also knew she couldn't hold out for long. She was a smart woman, practical. She would soon see that she couldn't go it alone, and he would be there, waiting to help her through. Just as he had promised his brother.

He would do this for anyone, he thought as he worked. It was good atonement to help others in need, but this held more importance. This was for David. Taking care of his brother's child was the last thing he would ever do for him.

"Hello?" A hesitant voice called from the doorway of the barn. Evie stepped inside.

"Good morning." He set down the bale of hay he had been moving and wiped the back of one arm across his brow, dislodging his hat with the motion. He settled it back onto his head proper.

"I brought you some coffee." She stopped and handed him the thermos she had tied around the handle of one of her crutches.

"Danki." He accepted the coffee and poured himself a portion in the lid. He blew across the top and took a tentative sip. Ah, that was good. "Clever trick," he said, nodding toward her crutches.

She shrugged and smiled. "We all do what we have to do."

"I suppose," he murmured. He wasn't sure of that at all. They all did what they had to do to survive, but too many hits and a person was down to the bare minimum just to keep going. He knew. He had lived there too long, existing each day. But Evie was different. She seemed to work with what she had without complaint or resentment. At least all the times he had seen her that was how she struck him—patient, loving and at peace with her lot in life.

That's God you're seeing in her.

He pushed that voice aside.

"Are you sticking around?" Evie asked.

"I'm not sure your sister wants me here."

"Can I tell you a secret?" She didn't wait for

him to answer. "My sister doesn't know what she wants. Or needs for that matter."

"Jah?" He wanted to press, but thought it better to allow her to tell him what was on her mind. If he asked too many questions, she might not reveal all that he needed to know.

"Mattie loved David."

He nodded. That much he already knew. "I'm glad my brother had someone like her in his life."

"Jah," she said. "It's going to take her some time to…come to terms with the fact that he's gone and her life is forever changed. Do you understand what I'm saying?"

"I think so, *jah.*"

"I was surprised that you came back to work today."

"Why's that?" He poured himself a second cup of coffee. He'd be all over the place after downing so much caffeine, but it was too good not to drink.

"She told us that you said you wanted to court her. We figured you'd come this morning to woo her."

"Woo her?"

Evie turned pink. "Something I read in a book. It's like courting."

He hid his smile. "I know what it is." But when was the last time he had heard anyone use that word? Come to think of it, had he ever?

"So you didn't?" she asked. "Come to woo her?"

He watched Evie closely, trying to get a feel for her thoughts. "I figured she needed a little time to get used to the idea." He gave a careless shrug, testing the waters once more.

"So you're not giving up?"

"Do you think I should?" He wasn't sure how much he should tell this sister. Was she a potential ally or a spy for the other side?

"No." The word was quiet and sweetly spoken. "I love my sister very much," she said. "But she can be a bit stubborn."

And prideful?

"She's only seeing her loss, not the consequences," Evie said. "It's to be expected. It's only been a few months."

He knew. He understood. He waited for her to continue.

"Give her some time," Evie advised. "But don't give up. Stay for lunch today."

He shook his head. As much as he would prefer to eat whatever deliciousness the women had planned as opposed to a cold can of whatever he had left in his duffel, they both knew he couldn't. "I shouldn't push it."

"You don't have to come into the house," she said. "We'll bring you out something. It's important that you stay."

"Yeah?" What was she planning? "I don't think that's what Mattie wants."

They both knew that to be the truth. But if Samuel was going to fulfill his promise, he was going to have to stick around whether Mattie wanted him there or not. That meant having some sort of plan. At that moment, he had none.

"She doesn't know what she wants or even needs right now."

"And what does she need?" Samuel asked.

Evie gave him a smile, so much like he remembered Mattie's from a lifetime ago. "Someone like you."

"We have one more for lunch," Evie chirped just after noon.

Mattie turned from getting the plates out of the cabinet and eyed her sister. "Why is that?" She set the plates down and faced her sister fully.

Evie didn't meet Mattie's gaze as she gave a small shrug. "Samuel is going to eat with us."

"You and I both know that he cannot come into this house and eat with us." She propped her hands on her hips and waited for her sister to explain.

"Then I'll take something out to him," Evie said simply.

Like it was simple at all.

"That's not any better." Mattie was a fool to even let him set foot on the property. She blamed the fact that he looked so much like David. It made her whimsical and soft. But the bishop was not one for shenanigans and as much as she knew of the definition of that word, Samuel on her farm definitely qualified. She was going to give him this one day, and then next time he came she would send him away. Immediately. *Jah*.

"The man's gotta eat."

That was true, but did he have to eat in her barn?

"Fine," she practically growled. "But I'll take it to him. You keep the girls inside." She didn't want them traumatized thinking their father had come back from the dead. "And after today, no more. Agreed?" She pressed Evie with a look.

"Agreed," Evie grumbled.

"I told you she would get like this."

Mattie spun around as Naomi entered the kitchen.

"You two are talking about me?"

"You are our sister," Naomi returned.

Mattie shook her head. "You're talking about me and Samuel," she corrected. "What is this? Some kind of romance intervention?"

Naomi sighed. "Romance has nothing to do with it."

She was all too aware. "You know what I mean."

Evie set the bundle of silverware on the table and came near. "Just give it some thought," she said quietly.

Why couldn't Evie have been bossy? Why did she have to be compassionate and caring? Mattie could have handled her younger sister trying to tell her what to do, but asking her...

"It's too soon." She gulped, swallowing back a sob as the tears threatened to fall. A heartbeat later she was surrounded by her sisters' arms, their love warming her from the inside out.

"We know," Naomi said.

"It's just so hard."

"We know that too," Evie murmured. "But there's more to think about." She gave Mattie another squeeze, then stepped back.

Naomi laid a gentle hand on Mattie's belly.

As if not wanting to be left out of the moment, the baby kicked the spot where her palm rested.

"Did you feel that?" Mattie asked, her tears threatening once again.

"That seals it." Evie nodded. "That's definitely a little Evie."

A baby girl to add to her all-female family. God willing.

"Baby Naomi," Naomi countered in a sing-song voice.

The three of them looked at one another and burst out laughing.

Mattie wiped tears of mirth from her eyes; at least they had started off that way. These days she could never be certain. One minute she was laughing and the next sobbing. But pregnancy and grief were a terrible combination.

She turned to Evie. "Go get the girls," she said. "I'll make him a plate."

Chapter Four

He could live to be a hundred years old and he would never understand women. He might as well give up trying now.

Samuel used a small piece of his bread to sop up anything left on his plate. It wasn't a habit he had picked up inside; it was something his *mamm* had instilled in him. Waste not, want not. And that was one thing that the Amish didn't do—waste food.

That had to have been the best meal he'd had since he'd gotten out. Even counting that truck stop just outside New Wilmington. He didn't know who made the food here, but apparently one of the sisters was a very good cook.

Sisters.

He had expected Evie to come out furtively bringing food to him. She had promised him "a plate," but he had imagined her shoving leftovers into her pockets in order to sneak it out to him.

Imagine his surprise when he saw Mattie herself standing in the doorway of the barn, holding a plate covered with a paper towel.

"We cannot make a habit of this," she had emphatically told him. "I appreciate your help, but after today—"

He nodded. After today he would have to think of some other reason to come by.

You should be concentrating on God. Getting back right with the church. How are you going to marry her if you are still under the Bann?

He had pushed that voice away, taken the plate from her with a quick smile and a thanks.

"Just leave it there," she had told him, pointing to the hay bale closest to the door. "One of us will come out and fetch it later"

After you've gone.

Don't come to the house.

Don't make it worse.

He read all this into her words and more.

Then she spun on her heel and quickly made her way back to the house.

So what was he doing now, standing on the front porch with the empty plate in one hand and his hat literally in the other? He said he was going to eat, then leave. He would go back to his campsite, maybe even try to get a glimpse of his mother. So many roads to travel before he would be back in good with the church, with his family. So many bridges to rebuild, so much forgiveness to ask for. So much pain ahead. But what choice did he have?

"Samuel?" Naomi's eyes widened with surprise. "I thought you'd be long gone by now."

He shook his head. "I just came to give you back your plate." He held it out to her.

"Danki," she said, stepping back and allowing him entrance to the house. "Come in, come in."

He hesitated. Wasn't this what he wanted? Maybe he stalled because he knew that Evie—and apparently Naomi—were on his side, but Mattie was a different story altogether. She wouldn't want him lingering in her living room. "I shouldn't."

"Come in," she said, her stern tone so much like her sister's.

He stepped into the house once again, feeling self-conscious. This was David's house. David's life. But Samuel had had a life of his own and he had lost it. No going back.

"It was a special treat," he told her with a small nod toward the plate. "I haven't had tomatoes that good in a long time." Especially not this close to the end of the year. After all, it was almost November.

"I've been raising tomatoes inside with a grow lamp." Evie came out of the kitchen and grinned. "The new plants are just now ready to bloom."

"Inside, you say?"

"Before David—" Evie stopped. "A few months ago, David set up a grow station in the basement so I could experiment raising vegetables indoors. Battery-operated lamps."

"*Dat* wouldn't let her do it at our house," Naomi put in. "You should see her. She tends those tomatoes like they're her own children."

Evie cupped one hand behind her ear. "I don't hear anyone complaining about having fresh tomatoes this late in the year."

"So I just ate homegrown tomatoes—" Samuel started.

"And we're supposed to get a hard freeze tonight," Evie finished for him. She was still smiling proudly.

"The man at the hardware store said it was going to snow."

The sisters whirled around as Mattie came out of the basement carrying two jars of what looked to be strawberry jam.

"Mattie." Naomi pressed a hand to her chest. "I didn't hear you come up."

"Obviously," Mattie drawled. "Here." She

handed the jars to Evie. "I'm guessing you wanted these for our uninvited guest."

"Well, uh," Evie stuttered. "*Jah.* I thought he might be able to use them. With some bread of course."

"Of course." Mattie raised one brow as if daring her sister to continue.

"It was my idea," Naomi said. "I thought it would be something nice for him to take to whoever he's staying with."

A dig for information if he had ever heard one.

"When were you in the hardware store?" Evie asked.

"Yesterday," Mattie replied. "When I went to get the paint and hinges."

"Right. For the chifforobe." Evie nodded.

"We bought a chifforobe at an auction a couple of weeks ago," Naomi explained.

"It needs new hinges on the doors," Evie added.

"And a coat of paint," Naomi put in.

"I can do it," Samuel said.

"No." Of course Mattie would protest his need to help.

"I don't mind and—" He cleared his throat. "You don't need to be messing around with paint."

"I wasn't planning to." She sniffed.

Evie shot him a sassy smile. "I'm going to paint it."

"*Jah*, okay." He gave a small nod.

"But I'm sure we can find something else for you to do," Naomi chimed in.

"Naomi!" Mattie screeched.

"What? The baby's room needs painting."

Mattie's green eyes went from wide with shock to narrowed in suspicion. "David just painted that room last year."

"Blue." Evie rolled her eyes. "You can't put a baby girl in a blue room."

"It's girl?" The words felt as if they had been squeezed from Samuel. It was bad enough they were talking about such matters in front of him, but that she was having a girl…

"We think it is," Naomi explained. "Baby Naomi."

"Little Evie," Evie countered; her eyes sparkled much like her sister's when she took a stand for the baby's name, so Samuel knew they were teasing. But a baby girl? What were the chances?

He shook the thought away. Fifty-fifty.

"She or *he* will be fine in a pale blue room. And this conversation needs to end."

Pregnancy was not something readily talked about in mixed company, and he could tell that Mattie was growing increasingly uncomfortable. It was him. He was the reason. If it were just her and her sisters, the conversation would rage on. But adding him into the mix…

"They call it *baby* blue for a reason." Evie rolled her eyes.

Samuel looked from one of them to the other. He had a feeling they were always like this. And it made him miss his brother all the more. But it was time to put the subject to rest.

"Mattie," he said quietly. "Do you want the room painted?"

She shook her head and a quiet, near somber air descended around them. "I don't think it matters."

"There's where you're wrong. It matters very much." He wanted to continue. *This is a very special baby and they need a very special room. If the very special mother wants it painted, then I'll paint it for her.* But he bit back the words knowing they were too intimate by far.

"Oohh," Evie gushed. "Pink. Like the color of baby lotion."

Samuel wanted to protest, but waited for Mattie to say something.

"If we can't put a baby girl in a blue room, then we surely can't put a baby boy in a pink room," she finally said, purposefully throwing her sister's words back at her.

"Hush," Naomi said. "You're going to jinx yourself into having a boy."

Samuel laughed, just a single chuckle. How long had it been since he had laughed at all? "I don't think that's possible."

Naomi shook her head, her mouth firm, her eyes teasing. "You never know. I wouldn't want to take that chance."

Samuel looked to Mattie for her answer. She was staring at her hands, clasped in front of her. Judging by the look on her face, she could have been thinking about anything from goats to tomatoes to the good Lord's blessings.

"How about a pale green?" Samuel managed to say. Green was a good color for both boys and girls, that much was certain. Emma always said so. What surprised him was that he had said the words at all.

Mattie raised her gaze, her eyes questioning. Had she heard something in his voice? "Not green," she whispered. It was as if she knew. "Yellow," she finally said. "The color of sunshine."

"Consider it done," Samuel replied. A moment passed between them. It was as if they were the only two in the room. Because they both loved David? Or something else? Most likely, he would never know. Then a voice sounded from the staircase and the moment was lost.

"No," Mattie finally said. "You're not supposed to be in the house now. You can't come in the house again. Not until— Not even—" She didn't finish the thought, but he knew. He shouldn't be in the house doing for her when he wasn't right with the church. But that was only a problem if the rest of the community knew he was there.

"I won't tell if you won't tell."

"No," she said once more.

"Mamm."

A small girl no more than three stood holding the hand of another, even smaller girl. Both had pigtails that ended in curls. The older one had green eyes just like her mother and blond hair with just a touch of red, but the younger...

Blue eyes, inky hair.

She was the spitting image of David. Of him. Of Sadie.

He pushed the thought from his mind, as his stomach clenched in recognition. David's girls. They had to be. Both of them. How had he not known that his brother had two daughters? How had he managed to let his family go to the point that he had been shut out? Whatever he had to do to get back in with his kin, that was what he would do. No matter how painful. The cost was the cost and he had to pay it.

"Is that…?" He nodded toward the girls, asking though he didn't need the answer. He could scarcely look at the smaller one. She was so much like his Sadie it brought stinging tears to his eyes. He blinked them away before anyone could notice.

Mattie pulled in a deep breath and frowned, her mouth turning in like she had been sucking on a lemon. Then she expelled the air and moved toward the girls.

"Dat," the oldest one said.

Here came those hot tears again. He fiercely blinked. He shouldn't be here. He hadn't known. They were too young. It was too confusing.

"No, *liebschdi*," Mattie said, scooping her younger daughter into her arms and grabbing the other by the hand.

He could see the anger in her gaze as she came near. And fear.

Evie and Naomi just watched to see what would happen.

"This is Samuel. He's your *dat*'s *brudder*."

"Not *Dat*," the girl repeated.

"No, baby. Not *Dat*."

Samuel's heart broke in two.

"Samuel, this is Gracie and Bethann." From her action, he noted that the younger was Gracie and the older Bethann and it wasn't lost on him that each girl bore at least a portion of Mattie's mother's name.

He nodded at both girls in turn. "It's nice to meet you," he said, his voice thick with regret, sadness and perhaps a little bit of joy. His brother might be gone, but he would live on through his girls.

"Now," she said, setting the toddler on her feet. "The two of you need to go play. While the grown-ups—" She shook her head. "Go play," she finished quietly.

"Jah, Mamm." Bethann took her sister's hand and guided her toward the stairs once more. She looked back at him one last time. "Not *Dat*," she said, then she turned and led her sister up the stairs and out of view.

"I hope you're happy."

Samuel turned, expecting to find Mattie pinning him with a hard gaze. Instead, she had it trained on her sisters.

"It was unavoidable," Naomi said, taking the defensive.

"No, it was not. And now—" She broke off as Samuel took a step forward. She whirled on him. "Go."

"Mattie, I—"

But she wasn't having it. Too much too soon. He knew.

"Go," she sternly repeated. "Now."

* * *

He was getting to her. Just not in the way he had hoped, but how was he supposed to know that she and David had two little ones? She had said nothing about it the day before. Just allowed him to muck the stalls and go about his day. Did she think that one good mucking would make him feel like he had done right by his brother?

No, he had promised to take care of David's family and as far as he was concerned that meant marriage. He knew that was what David had meant. But how was he supposed to marry his twin brother's widow when two little children couldn't tell the difference between him and their dead father? It was unbearable to think about.

Samuel kicked a rock at the side of the road. He wanted to kick more, punch something, yell, scream, do anything to release all this pressure building up inside. If he were anywhere else, he would strap on some running shoes and take off across the fields that lay dormant this time of year. He'd run until he couldn't run any longer, then he would run some more.

Fat Eddie used to always tell him that he couldn't outrun his problems and maybe that was true. But at least he felt better after a run. The tension released and the pressure eased and things got back into focus. But he didn't think anyone in Millers Creek would understand an Amish man running across the valley for no other reason than to run. And Fat Eddie was still back in McKean.

As he approached a hill, Samuel saw the black top of the buggy before the horse came into view. He ducked off the road and hid behind a tree. A black buggy meant someone from another church district and not his own, but Millers Creek wasn't that big and the black toppers and the yellow toppers, or the Reno Amish and the Byler Amish, all knew each other. If he was spotted, then word would get around that he was home before he was ready to let everyone know.

And Mattie?

He was taking a chance with her, for sure, but with her reluctance to let him help, he was fairly certain she would keep his presence to herself. He hoped anyway. It was a chance he was willing to take, and truthfully, only then because he knew he was going to have to come clean eventually. Tell the bishop he was back. Ask for his path to rejoin the *gmee*. Call on his family and accept the rejection he knew was sure to come. But only then would he be able to overcome their objections and set his life back right.

Your life was right.

It had been, but now it hadn't been for a long time. Things were different. He was different.

Once the buggy moved past, Samuel came back to the side of the road. Only a few more yards to the farm road that led to his camp. It was supposed to get cold tonight. One of the reasons that he had taken the blanket from Mattie's barn. He hadn't stolen it, just borrowed it. He had been meaning to ask her, but then after the girls...

It just didn't seem right. But the weather was taking a turn and he had to be prepared.

He ambled down the narrow road, praying all the while that no one would see him. There was a chance that one of his brothers might be out and about and happen to spot him. He could only pray that it didn't happen until he was ready.

The small blue tent was strung between two trees. He didn't have a campfire, nor anything to cook with. So he'd saved a piece of the bread from his lunch to have tonight. He had a little bit of beef jerky left and a couple of those little mandarin oranges. It wasn't a lot, but it would keep his stomach from rumbling all night long. And tomorrow he would see about restocking a bit with whatever money he had left. It wasn't much, but surely, he could make it another couple of days. After that, he wasn't sure what he would do. Maybe by then he'd be ready to face his *mudder*.

He thought of the jars of strawberry jam that Mattie had held and the promise of the bread that Evie had mentioned. The bread that he could smell the minute he stepped foot on her porch. His stomach grumbled with the memory. He had walked off without it. What he had in his camp would have to do for tonight.

Samuel tossed the wool blanket into the tent and pulled his collar up a little closer around his neck. He didn't have a coat. He wasn't sure what had happened to his Amish jacket when he had left. Who was to know? It was gone. Now all he had between him and the incoming cold front was a thin blue shirt and a fleece hoodie, a sleeping bag and a contraband blanket that he prayed its owner wouldn't notice was gone before he could return it.

Samuel pulled the jacket from his duffel and shoved his arms into the sleeves. He zipped it up and crawled into the tent. Dark was a long way off, but what else did he have to do but lie in there and hope that everything turned out the way it was supposed to?

He grabbed his pencil and his crossword puzzle and started to work.

Mattie stood at the window and watched as the wispy snowflakes fell. It was the first of November and they were already having snow. It was going to be some winter. Not that the snow was sticking. That it was snowing at all was the strange thing.

"I think he's still coming," Evie said from beside her.

Mattie turned toward her sister. "Who?"

"Really?" Evie asked. "That's how you want to be?" Her teasing smile took the sting from her words.

"I don't know what you're talking about." When had she started telling such lies?

"Give him a chance," Evie said after a moment. "He only wants to help."

He wanted much more than that, and they both knew it.

"If the bishop finds out he's been coming here—"

"Which he won't unless you tell him. I'm not telling him. I'm pretty sure Naomi and Samuel aren't telling him. That leaves you." Evie gave her a pointed look.

Another lie. This one by omission.

She had tried to send him away, but she didn't have the energy to do much more than that. She had her girls to think about, the baby, her farm. She couldn't spare much effort for a man who would eventually give up and move on. Let him get back right with the church. That was the most important thing. Maybe by then he would give up his crazy idea of a promise to his brother and instead start his life with someone else.

"There he is." Evie smiled as she said the words. Mattie couldn't see what there was to smile about. He was trouble for her. She knew it, and she had been praying against hope that he wouldn't come today. That the snow would keep him in wherever he was staying. But she should have known better. The man was Amish. He was used to working in any conditions. He might have left the community for a while, but some things couldn't be forgotten.

Mattie ignored the lurch her heart gave. It was ridiculous that she had reacted at all to seeing him. Samuel was nothing more than a carbon copy of David. A fact that she had to remind herself of every time he was near. Her heart beat a little faster in her chest until she told herself that the man she was looking at was Samuel and not her beloved David.

"What's he wearing?" Evie asked, squinting as she looked out the window.

"Maybe you should wear your glasses more," Mattie said.

"I don't like them," Evie returned. "So what's he got on?"

"One of those sweatshirt jackets with a hood," Mattie replied. Not the Amish coat she would have expected. She had known that he had left the Amish and lived among the *Englisch* a little. That much had been common knowledge in Millers Creek for years, but to see him in Amish dress and not Amish outerwear was a little bit shocking. It only proved the rumors were true.

"He'll freeze out there in that."

That's his problem. She wanted to say those words, but they wouldn't budge from her brain. They stuck there as if too barbed to come loose. She wanted not to care. She didn't want him to be her concern. He shouldn't be her concern and yet...

"What do you have in here that he can wear?"

"Nothing," she answered, even though she knew it wasn't the truth. There was one thing...

"What's going on?" Naomi came out of the downstairs bathroom, both girls cleaned up from breakfast, dressed and ready to start their day. How she relied on Naomi to help her with the two of them.

Evie moved away from the window and toward the pegs next to the door. The ones that held their winter coats. "Samuel's here," she said. "And he's wearing a flimsy jacket."

"Isn't it snowing?" Naomi asked.

Bethann clapped her hands. "Snow."

"That's right." Naomi smiled at her niece. Bethann was standing by her side while she cradled Gracie on one hip. "I don't think it'll last though. But we'll have others."

"Snow," Bethann said again.

"How about this?" Evie held up David's coat.

"No." She didn't think about the word. Or how callous it sounded to let her brother-in-law work outside on her farm and practically freeze to death when she could do something about it.

"It's a coat," Evie said.

And it was. It was just a coat that she would need to give away soon. But she hadn't had the heart to do it. Not yet anyway. She wasn't ready. Maybe because she didn't have his summer hat. A hat was an easy thing to keep and have always. But a coat took up more room, hung in the way. A constant reminder...

Something he would never wear again.

"Fine." Her heart broke as she said the word, but she was getting used to the pain. She moved back quickly from the window as Samuel came up onto the porch.

He skipped up the steps like he owned the place and knocked confidently on the door.

Mattie turned to Naomi as Evie moved to answer it. "Take them—" *into the kitchen, the bedroom, the bathroom, anyplace but there.*

Naomi bounced Gracie on her hip. "Come on," she said, grabbing Bethann's hand. "Let's go play." Without another word, Evie and Mattie waited until she had led them up the stairs.

Once they were out of sight, Evie nodded toward Mattie, then opened the door. "Samuel." Her voice rang with surprised greeting as if they hadn't been watching him the entire time he walked up the driveway.

"I just wanted to let you know that I was here."

Mattie stepped forward. "You didn't have to come today." She would have preferred him to have not. But there he was.

"I was going to fix the fence over by the milking barn. I'm surprised the goats haven't been getting out."

"I fixed it," Mattie said. Maybe not as good as David would have done, but good enough that even the cleverest of her goats couldn't escape.

"Since yesterday?" he asked.

She slowly shook her head, her prayer *kapp* strings brushing against her neck. The sensation made her want to shiver and she squelched the urge. "Before yesterday."

He nodded. "I see. Well, I'm going to work on it a bit. You never can be too careful with goats." And that was a truth she couldn't argue with.

"Here." Evie stepped forward, her crutches clanking as she extended David's coat toward him.

"What's this?" he asked.

"A coat," Evie said simply. "For you to wear. It's too cold out there to wear only a jacket."

"Thank you," he said.

Mattie could feel his gaze on her as he trailed his fingers over the black wool.

"Are you sure?" he asked.

He knew it had belonged to David.

She nodded without looking up. Wasn't it enough that she had given her consent?

"I really appreciate it," he murmured. "I'll be in the barn if anyone needs me."

She didn't need him. Not for anything. Not to paint the baby's room, not to muck out the stalls, not to fix the fence. And especially not to marry her.

Mattie moved toward the kitchen, pretending to have chores to do there. So she heard rather than saw him leave, and Evie closed the door behind him.

She would get through this. He had to give up soon. He would learn that she didn't need him. She didn't want him. He might need the forgiveness of the rest of the *gmee*, but he didn't have to get it from her.

She went to the cabinet and started taking down the flour, sugar and other ingredients for a cake. Or maybe some banana bread. Something. She needed to bake something to have a task for her hands and mind. They didn't need a cake or sweet bread. Evie had made a cherry pie the day before. They had been finishing up the rest of a pan of lemon squares at supper and the pie was still resting whole and uncut on the sideboard.

She stopped, started loading the ingredients back into the cabinet. No sense in being wasteful and extravagant just because she was having trouble dealing with the reality of the situation.

Her husband's twin was insisting on helping her, to assuage his own guilt for being gone.

"Mattie." Evie's voice carried to her, a little too high and filled with trepidation. "Someone's here."

"Jah," she said. "Samuel."

"No," Evie called in return. "Someone else. And it looks like the bishop's wife."

Chapter Five

"What?" Mattie rinsed her hands and grabbed her apron to dry them. Then she thought better of the action and snatched up a dishtowel before hurrying out of the kitchen. "What's Eleanor Peachey doing here?"

"I don't know," Evie said. "But it looks like you're about to find out."

Hilarious.

"Is that—" Naomi came rushing down the stairs, Gracie on one hip and Bethann right behind. She didn't need to finish for Mattie to know what she was about to say.

"*Jah.* Can you put on some water for coffee?"

"What does she want?" Naomi asked.

"How am I supposed to know?" Mattie shot back. But she could guess, and she was pretty certain it had something to do with Samuel Byler. It seemed everything led back to him these days.

Or maybe Eleanor just wanted to visit for a spell.

Not very likely.

"Naomi," she called. "Coffee?"

"Right." Naomi flew the rest of the way down the stairs and toward the kitchen. Her free hand fluttered to her prayer covering. She was always so busy, hurrying from one chore to another that her *kapp* seemed perpetually crooked.

"It's fine," Mattie said, but she made her way over to Naomi and tugged on one side. "This wouldn't happen if you used more pins."

"Or tied it under your chin," Evie teased.

"Hush that," Naomi said. "Is it okay now?"

Gracie patted one chubby hand on the side of Naomi's *kapp*.

Naomi smiled at her niece.

"Coffee?" Mattie prompted

"Coffee," Naomi repeated with a nod. Her *kapp* slipped a bit as she turned.

Mattie looked to Evie, who only shook her head. But she was smiling. There were a few things that Mattie could always count on her sisters for: smiles, hugs and unconditional support.

"And put Gracie in her high chair and Beth-ann at the table. They can play with the salt dough."

"Got it," Naomi responded.

Mattie turned to Evie. "I need you to do something."

"Jah?"

"Go out into the barn. Tell Samuel to stay out of sight."

"Good thinking."

Hopefully he had seen the buggy pull up and was not planning on coming out anytime soon.

"Where's Charlie?" Mattie asked. Why in times of stress did it seem like the mischievous animal always disappeared?

"She was on the couch a moment ago," Evie said. "She can't be far."

Mattie shook her head. She couldn't run the animal down now. It was only a matter of time before—

A knock sounded on the front door.

"Just warn Samuel."

"Of course." Evie moved toward the door.

"Eleanor," Evie greeted.

Charlie picked that time to run out from under the coffee table where she had been hiding. She flew past Evie and straight through Eleanor's legs.

"Whoo!" The bishop's wife squealed as the goat rushed past.

"I'll just…" Evie pointed the end of one crutch toward the door as the bishop's wife stepped into the house.

"Jah," Mattie said. "You do that."

"You're going after that animal in this weather?"

"Somebody's got to get her." Evie shared a look with Mattie.

"But—" Eleanor started, wanting to state the obvious but understandably not wanting to broach such a delicate subject. How was a girl who needed crutches to walk going to chase down a wayward goat? A goat, Mattie was sure, Eleanor felt belonged outside with the rest of Mattie's herd.

"I've got it." Evie nodded in that stubborn way she had.

That was Evie, independent as they come. But Mattie couldn't fault her for that. She'd had a tough time of it, wanting to run and play with the other children and unable to do so. Now her best friend, Freeman, was getting married. Mattie needed to get herself together because Evie was going to need all the love and sisterly support soon. Freeman and Helen were supposed to get married in January. Of course, Evie thought that no one knew her true feelings for her friend, but sisters have a way.

Mattie sent her sister a tight smile. "The treats are in the barn." Then she turned to the bishop's wife. "That goat will follow anyone as long as they have a bag of dried sweet potato chips."

"Humph." Eleanor frowned, but thankfully didn't say anything else.

"So," Mattie said, closing the door quietly behind her sister, "what brings you out on a day like this?"

The bishop's wife shook the light snow from her boots. "It's not so bad out there," she said as she removed her bonnet then hung it on a peg by the door.

David's black wool winter hat still hung there. Mattie should find someone who needed it and pass it on. Or maybe she would keep it for her girls.

"Did someone tell you that Evie baked a cherry pie yesterday afternoon?" Mattie asked as she forced a smile.

"Is that a fact?" Eleanor loved cherry pie and everyone in the district knew it.

"It is at that," Naomi said, stepping out from the kitchen. "You want me to cut you a slice?"

"I can't stay," Eleanor protested.

"Not even for pie?" Mattie teased, all the while hoping she would turn it down.

Mattie could see the indecision on Eleanor's face. She wanted to stay—she wanted to eat pie—but she was probably getting tired of letting all her clothes out. She had gained a few pounds in the last year. Like most Amish women she worked from sunup to sundown, but now all of her children were out of the house.

All except for Wally, her youngest, and Mattie had heard rumors that Eleanor's daughter, the recently widowed Ellen King, might be moving back in with her two *kinner.* Still, with most of the children out of the house, there wasn't as much work to do as there had been before. Same food intake, less work meant a few extra pounds. And then there was a fondness for sweets, say cherry pie.

"Let me take your cape," Mattie said. If it took the bishop's wife this long to refuse, then she was fairly certain Eleanor wasn't going to.

The woman gave a sheepish grin and removed her cape just as Naomi came back into the room with a tray. She had a coffee urn, four cups and four pieces of pie. And Evie was still outside.

"I want pie," Bethann called from her place at the nearby dining table.

Gracie smacked her hands against the high chair tray and squealed her agreement.

"Just a minute," she called to the girls. Then Mattie took the cape from Eleanor and started to hang it on the peg next to her bonnet.

There was David's hat. She took it down, replaced it with the cape, then turned to find all eyes on her. She wanted to ask what they were looking at, but she wasn't sure she was prepared for the answer.

Instead, she moved to the hall closet and placed David's hat on the shelf there. It would be out of the way—out of sight—until she could find something to do with it.

She turned back to her sister and the bishop's wife. "Split mine between the girls," she told Naomi.

Her sister nodded. Thankfully, she hadn't gotten out the salt clay yet. So she moved toward the table with the large piece of pie.

Bethann did a fair enough job feeding herself, but Gracie was as independent as her aunt. She would feed herself only to have most of the pie end up in her hair. She would need a bath after the bishop's wife left.

Maybe they would get to making the star garland for Christmas after that. Or maybe it would have to wait until tomorrow.

Mattie moved to David's chair and sat. It still smelled like him. Or maybe it was just her memory holding on. "So, Eleanor, what brings you out today?"

Eleanor settled down on the couch and accepted the small plate with a large piece of cherry pie in the middle. She cleared her throat. "I just came by to see how you were getting along."

"Fine," Mattie said. "Just fine." She took a sip of her coffee as if that somehow proved the truth in her words. She squelched a grimace. She preferred it with sugar, but her sister had left the sweeteners in the kitchen.

"*Jah.* Well." Eleanor looked down at the tray.

Naomi had moved back from giving the girls Mattie's slice of pie and taken up her own plate. Pie and coffee had been distributed and still one piece sat on the tray.

Eleanor cleared her throat again.

Mattie took another small sip of the coffee and waited for the bishop's wife to continue.

"I heard that Samuel Byler has come back to town."

News traveled fast—good and bad, though Mattie wasn't sure which one this was.

"Is that so." Mattie took another drink of the coffee and wondered how she should play this. She was his twin's widow. Of course he would come to see her. She had known him practically her entire life. The valley wasn't that big.

"I also heard that he might be coming around to see you."

"I see." Not quite an answer, but it gave her an extra heartbeat to decide how to answer the direct question she knew was coming next.

"Is that true?"

"He may have been by a couple of times."

Eleanor took a bite of her pie and shifted in her seat as she chewed.

Mattie couldn't tell if she was moving around because she liked the pie so much or she was anxious to continue talking.

"I know he's your husband's brother and all, but…"

"But what?" Mattie kept her voice quiet and level. No sense getting worked up for what she had known all along.

"He's not right with the church," Eleanor began.

"I know this. And I've done my best to keep him at a distance while trying to hear him out. He's grieving as well."

Eleanor nodded. "*Jah*. Well. There's more to it than that."

"Really?" Calm and level. This was the part Eleanor was getting to all along.

"I have a friend, Becky, who lives out in western Pennsylvania. In New Wilmington where Samuel lived. And there's something amiss."

"Amiss?" Mattie asked.

Eleanor nodded. "He's not what he appears to be."

The words sent a pang zinging through Mattie's middle. But she ignored it and the tingle it spread to her fingers. The fact of the matter was that Eleanor was the biggest gossip in Millers Creek. She was the first one to say a rumor and the last one to repeat it. If she had heard something...

If she has heard something, it's probably true.

The front door opened before Eleanor could explain. Evie came in, leading Charlie on a length of rope she had obviously taken from the barn.

"This goat," she said with a shake of her head. She removed the loop from around Charlie's neck, then brushed the snow from her shoulders.

"Is it sticking?" Mattie asked. It was bad enough that it was snowing.

Her goats hated the cold and spent almost all their time indoors during the winter months. David had set up a shed with shelves for them to climb on and sleep on, though no one knew that would be the end result when he had begun. She had learned a lot about the peculiar habits of goats over the years. He had also rigged up a small propane-fueled heater to warm the building. The only problem with that was getting them out of that building and into the milking parlor when the cold hit.

"No," Evie said. "And the goats are fine."

The way she said this last indicated that she wasn't talking about the goats at all. Not really. She was talking about Samuel. At least now Mattie knew that he wouldn't accidentally get caught on the property by the bishop's wife. It was one thing to tell her that he came and she sent him away and quite another for her to find him there mucking stalls or some such.

"Now," Eleanor started again. She took another bite of pie and balanced the small plate on her knee. "As I was saying…"

Charlie picked that moment to jump onto the couch next to her. The crazy goat began to delicately nibble on the crust of the cherry pie. Then she all out started lapping up the gooey cherry middle.

"Well, I have never—" Eleanor jumped to her feet, dumping the pie onto the floor with a small splat and a matching clatter of plate and fork.

Charlie hopped to the ground and returned to munching away at the treat, nudging the saucer out of the way with her nose.

"Eleanor, I—" Mattie was on her feet too, but unable to finish the statement. She what?

Beside her, Naomi slapped one hand over her mouth and stifled her bark of laughter. Evie coughed to hide her own. Gracie squealed and splatted her hands in the remains of her pie while Bethann slid from her seat to come squat next to her pet. "Charlie likes pie."

"For the life of me—" Eleanor started again. She shook her head and marched toward the door. "Be careful," she said, pointing a sharp finger at Mattie. "That man is under the *Bann* for a reason. Remember that next time he comes callin'." She donned her bonnet and cape, eyes blazing the entire time.

Mattie knew she should apologize, for something—the goat hopping onto the couch, the goat stealing her pie, maybe even having a goat as a pet—but she could not bring out the words to do so. Instead, she simply watched as the bishop's wife prepared to leave.

"*Danki* for stopping by," she managed. She forced a polite smile and opened the door. A blast of cold air came in as, thankfully, Eleanor walked out. "Be safe."

Eleanor harumphed, then made her way down the steps and toward her waiting buggy.

Mattie shut the door and resisted the urge to hold it closed lest Eleanor decide to come back and demand a second piece of pie. She did, however, lean against it and waited to hear the rattle of the reins and the clomp of the horse's hooves as Eleanor left. Only when the sound faded to nothing did she breathe a sigh of relief.

"What was that about?"

Mattie whirled around to find Samuel standing in the doorway from the kitchen.

"How did you get in here?" she screeched.

He jerked one thumb over his shoulder. "Back door."

"Of course."

"Not *Dat*." Bethann rose from her place next to Charlie and made her way over to him.

Mattie noticed he swallowed hard before responding to the girl. "Samuel." He pointed toward himself.

She stuck her own thumb on her chest and smiled proudly at him. "Befann."

"Nice to see you again."

Mattie pulled herself together and started toward him. "You can't be here."

"I know, I just—"

He just what? Wanted to hear what the bishop's wife knew about him?

What had Eleanor been about to tell her concerning Samuel Byler? Mattie might never know. Did she really want to know?

"Samuel Byler." Mattie shooed him back toward the kitchen door. "Get yourself right with the church. And don't come back until you do."

Chapter Six

Samuel stood at the edge of the road, just before the lane that led to his father's house. Truly, his father had been gone for years now, but Samuel would always consider the white clapboard two-story as belonging to Aaron Byler.

All he had to do was go up and knock. Tell his family, his mother, why he had come home. Well, maybe not all of the why, but that he was home for good and was going to get his life back in order. An order they would understand and approve of.

If he only had the courage.

The problem was, as much as he considered the house Aaron Byler's, so did its inhabitants. They would uphold Aaron's decision and declaration that Samuel was dead to the family. If only he could get them to change their minds.

Time. He knew it would take time. Probably

even more than he truly had. But what choice did he have but to try?

His knees shook as he walked past the line of trees that separated the house from the main road. The bright yellow church wagon was set off to one side, testament that worship would be at their house the following Sunday.

Two dogs lay in the shade of the trees, barely lifting their heads as he walked by. Obviously, they weren't for security. An orange tabby cat met him halfway. He meowed and sniffed Samuel's pant leg, then headbutted him as he started to purr.

"Hi, there." Samuel bent down to pet the cat's large head. This was probably the best greeting that he was going to get. He might as well soak it up and store those good feelings for the confrontation to come.

Then again, maybe time had softened his mother's heart. Maybe time had loosened the hold that Aaron Byler had over his wife. Maybe time had brought about forgiveness.

Maybe she would invite him in.

"That's far enough."

Maybe not.

"Mamm."

The years had added to his *mudder*. A few extra pounds, a few more gray hairs and a few more wrinkles. But she was a welcome sight. Comforting, even as she frowned at him.

"You can't be here." She crossed her arms and squared off her feet as if daring him to come closer.

"I'm back," he said, then realized that it was no answer at all. "I mean to stay."

"Jah." She didn't sound convinced.

"I'm going to talk to the bishop soon. I'm going to straighten everything out with the church and—"

"Come back when you do." She turned, disappeared back into the house and left him standing there. He would like to think that he had seen a bit of hope in her eyes. Hope and possibly forgiveness, but he knew better. Aaron Byler's hold on his family was strong and it would take a little more than unfulfilled promises to change that.

Samuel shifted his stance, crossed his arms, then uncrossed them and shifted again. "Just tell me what it is I can do." He watched the play of emotions across Mattie's face, the hope, the fear, the resignation, then the stubbornness.

"You can leave," she said. "I told you not to come back until you had everything right with the church. I can't have you here."

But the truth was he knew that she would be

acting the same if he was okay with the church. She was just that independent. If he had already bent his knee, confessed his sins and asked for forgiveness, nothing would be different between the two of them. If only getting himself back in the good graces of his community were that simple. It might not automatically change things between him and Mattie, but it would definitely be a start in the right direction.

"I thought with the rain…"

A low mist had started after the snow. Samuel wasn't sure which was worse when outside squatting at the edge of his mother's property in a tent he had picked up in a secondhand store. The thin nylon wasn't much protection from either, but he supposed at least the temperature had risen enough that the snow became rain. As the son of a farmer, rain was always good. Except when squatting at the edge of someone else's property in a secondhand tent.

He had shivered all night. Even his socks felt damp. Yeah, they needed the rain, especially before the winter set in. Snow wasn't quite as nourishing to the land. It had its benefits though. It helped insulate the crops and provided nitrogen to the soil. But he would rather have had the snow after he had found a more permanent place to live. Yet with the reception he'd had from his mother yesterday, that time might be well into the future.

"Tell me what I can do," he asked again. It was the same question he had asked her countless times that morning. Mainly because by the time he got to her house, she had already done the majority of the chores. Including mucking out the stalls and milking the goats. He had only managed to help her haul extra bales of hay into the building the goats used as sort of a…goat barn.

He didn't know what to call it. It was a large building where the goats could go to get out of the elements. There were shelves and hay and a heater. Come to find out, goats didn't like the cold very much. His *dat* had had a couple of goats when they were growing up, mostly just to eat the grass and the leftovers and not for anything special. So he didn't know as much about goats. But he was willing to learn.

Yet since he arrived today, all he had done was follow Mattie around, watching her lift lids on canisters in the main barn and bite her lip as if a great dilemma had been presented to her.

"I need Evie." She crossed her arms as if daring him to contradict her.

Samuel threw his hands up in surrender and marched toward the house.

Well, *marched* was a really strong word. Considering how soft the ground was and how many mud puddles there were between where he and Mattie had been standing in front of the regular barn and over to the stairs that led to the porch. He made his way up to the front door and knocked.

All in all, his miserable night was turning into an equally miserable morning.

He looked back at Mattie as he waited for one of the sisters to answer the door. From the time it took, he supposed that Evie herself would arrive at any moment.

Mattie stood where he left her, still biting her lip and frowning as if trying to decide what to do. Maybe he would be able to help her if she would just let him know what it was. But no, she wanted to stand on the ceremony of the rules of their community and not let him help her because he was under the *Bann*.

What was wrong? And why wouldn't she tell him?

He turned back to the door just as it was opened. As he had suspected, Evie stood there. The door had only been open a second before Mattie's pygmy goat darted out between her feet.

"Whoa, there." He scooped her up in his arms before she even got all four feet onto the porch.

The goat *mahed* in return.

She really was a petite little thing, smaller than even some of the medium-sized dog breeds, but it seemed maybe twice as mischievous.

"Charlie!" Evie admonished.

Samuel looked down at the goat he held in his arms. She was white except for her feet, which were as black as coal. She also had a few random smudges here and there, like on the edges of her ears and one little line under her nose. "I get it," he said. "Charlie. Like Charlie Chaplin."

Evie frowned at him. "Who?"

Samuel shook his head. "Never mind."

She nodded, stood there for a moment just looking at him. Then he realized he was the one who'd knocked on the door, and it hadn't been to talk about the goat. "Right," he said. "Mattie needs you. I don't know what for. She won't tell me."

Evie didn't look a bit surprised. "Just put Charlie in the house." She stepped out onto the porch, leaving Samuel to move around her to get the goat back inside.

"You're not going to—" he started, but then thought better of it. He had been about to say *go out in all that mud*, but she was a grown woman. She could make the decision on getting dirty or not. And whether or not she might have trouble navigating all the mud with braces and crutches…well, it really had nothing to do with him.

"What?" she asked.

He shook his head. "Never mind."

He set the goat in the house and shut the door quickly behind her so that she didn't have even a half a heartbeat to escape. By the time he turned around, Evie was standing at the top of the stairs, and Mattie at the bottom.

"I need you to go to the feed store and get some more food for the goats." Was that a note of dejection he heard in her tone?

"What happened?" He looked from Evie to Mattie and back again.

"That's what I want to know," Evie said.

Mattie pressed her lips together. She didn't want to answer him. But since he had asked a direct question, she didn't have much choice. Or maybe she did. But since Evie had asked her as well…

"There's a leak in the roof of the barn and it dripped on the goat feed. It's ruined."

"Do you think he has another barrel of it?"

"What kind of feed are we talking about here?" Samuel asked.

Both women ignored him. "He knows we've been using it," Mattie said.

"Jah," Evie agreed, "but you just bought that

one barrel, and he had to special order that. Do you think he has another?"

"Is this some kind of special feed?" Samuel asked.

Mattie pinched the bridge of her nose between her thumb and forefinger. She closed her eyes. She looked like she was getting a headache. Not that he could blame her. But she seemed to worry entirely too much about things out of her control.

"I could stop by the phone shanty and call," Evie offered.

Mattie continued to pinch her nose even as she nodded. "That's a good idea."

"Is that the only place in town that sells the feed?" Samuel asked.

"Let me get my coat and my purse." Evie turned back toward the door.

"Are you really going to get out in this weather?" Samuel asked.

Evie looked at him and frowned. "It's not raining or snowing anymore."

"But—" Samuel broke off as Mattie shook her head. Oh, *now* she wanted to talk to him.

"*Danki*, Evie," Mattie said, still pinning Samuel with a lethal look.

Evie stopped, one hand on the doorknob as she turned back to look between the two of them. A glance at Mattie's face, a glance at Samuel's face, then she shook her head and opened the door.

"If you're going to insist on hanging around," Mattie started, her tone threaded with steel, "then you need to learn that Evie treasures her independence. Don't you do anything to take it away from her."

Samuel felt immediately remorseful. "I didn't mean to. I—"

"It doesn't matter whether you meant to or not. You treat her just as you would treat Naomi. Got it?"

"I got it," he said. "I meant no harm."

"I know you didn't. But the fact still remains—" It was her turn to break off as Evie came back out of the house.

It took everything Samuel had to stand on the porch and watch her make her way through the muddy yard and over to the barn.

"I'll get the carriage out for you," Mattie called.

"*Danki*, sister," Evie said as she disappeared inside the barn.

"What is the difference in you getting the carriage out and me helping her by going and getting the food?"

"Really?" Mattie said. "You're going to question the logic of a woman?"

Samuel closed his eyes. "Right. My bad," he said. "I'll get the carriage out."

Mattie shook her head. "Not on your life."

Mattie's patience was stretched as thin as one-pound fishing line by the time Evie was in the carriage and on her way to the feed store. She wasn't sure exactly what was bothering her so much. Or maybe it was just a combination of things. The fact that Samuel had showed up again today even after she had told him not to. The fact that she had to get up two hours early because she knew in her heart that he was going to show up even though he had promised not to. Or maybe it was the rain.

She couldn't deny that they needed the moisture. Or that the rain was good for everything from the grass that she allowed her goats to eat to the garden full of organic vegetables she grew for them in their pasture each year. All of that would grow better in the spring with good rain in the winter. Or maybe it was just Samuel trying to help and somehow crushing all their feelings beneath the soles of his boots in the process.

"So I take it you don't feed your goats table scraps?"

Mattie whirled around, the mud sucking at her muck boots as she did so. "Table scraps?"

"You say that like I said poison hemlock."

"I should think not," she said, wondering what she had done in the past couple of weeks to warrant having such a trying time now. Hadn't she been through enough? "They're both equally bad for them."

Or rather equally bad for her business. *Jah*, goats could eat about three ounces of poison hemlock without showing signs of the toxicity, but table scraps would absolutely ruin her organic certification.

"I see." But the two words clearly indicated that he did not.

Mattie closed her eyes briefly then opened them again and pinned her brother-in-law with a stare. "If you're going to insist on coming here and helping out—"

He opened his mouth as if to interrupt, so she held up a finger to stay his words.

"If you insist on coming here, then you need to learn a few things about the business."

"Finally," he said, a relieved smile creeping on to his lips. "This is what I've been trying to get to all along." His look was so smug, and she was having none of that.

"The first thing you need to know about this business is it's mine and you need to keep out of it."

"Mattie," he called after her as she marched

into the barn. She didn't stop to see what he wanted.

He would follow her regardless, she knew.

He caught up with her just inside the tack room.

She heard him come in and kept her back to the door. She just needed a moment to get herself together. But with Samuel, it seemed, that was another impossibility. She blinked away her tears but stubbornly kept her back to him.

"I just want to help."

His words were so quietly and gently spoken, that she couldn't take it anymore. All the emotions that she'd been pushing down for days, weeks, some for even months rose to the surface and threatened to choke her. Hot tears spilled from her lashes. But she let them fall knowing that if she reached out to brush them aside, he would know she was crying. And that was the last thing she wanted.

The last thing—the very last thing—she wanted was this man's pity. That was what it was all about. It all boiled down to this promise that he had supposedly made to David. It was all about pity. He pitied her. He pitied that his brother was gone and that she had two daughters and another baby on the way. That she would be raising them all by herself.

So in steps super brother Samuel to save the

day. Well, she wasn't about to be on the receiving end of a pity promise. She wanted to tell him so. She wanted to whirl around and lay into him. She wanted to give him the what for, and as her grandmother used to say, tell him how the cow ate the cabbage. But she just didn't have the strength anymore.

"Mattie?"

Her name was a whisper on his lips as if he somehow knew that if he said it any louder it would break whatever thread was connecting them. And there was a connection. That was another thing tearing her heart to shreds, even as she reminded herself that he looked identical to her husband. Of course she would have feelings when she saw him. There was no way around it. She had been walking around knowing that her husband was dead these past four months and now Samuel had shown up wearing his face, and now his coat. How was she supposed to keep those feelings from completely washing over her?

"Go away, Samuel." She said the words, but she knew they would be ineffective. She told him that yesterday and the day before and the day before that. But now she didn't really mean for him to leave the farm, she just wanted him to leave her alone and give her a chance to pull herself back together. Being strong was no joke.

"Mattie, I—" His fingers on her arm were gentle. As much as she hated to admit it, his touch was both warm and familiar and somewhat welcome. But for all its familiarity, something in it was different, though she couldn't lay her finger on just what it was. She didn't have the strength to fight him as he turned her around to face him.

"Why are you crying?" he asked. His tone wasn't accusing, but concerned as if he were asking what reason did she have to cry at all.

But she needed that insensitivity to fuel her anger. She jerked away from him. "Why am I crying? *Why* am I crying?"

"That's not what I meant," he started. But there was no way she was letting him finish now. She had gotten her legs back under her and there was no going back.

"I tell you what, Samuel Byler. You figure it out and then you can tell me." And with that she whirled on her heel and stomped out of the barn.

He called her name once, twice, but she didn't stop. She continued across the yard, up the porch steps and into the house.

She barely caught Charlie before the goat darted out the door, then she slammed it behind her and leaned back against it.

Safe. Finally safe.

Chapter Seven

A smart man knew when to cut his losses and head home. Truth be known, he didn't always consider himself a smart man. In this case, however, he was half of one. He left Mattie's farm, deciding he would give her time to cool off and whatever else she needed to do to get herself back together. He felt bad about her tears. He supposed he just pushed too hard. That was what happened when you weren't in polite society for the better part of four years. You forgot how to act. Or at least he had. So he had left, and that in itself made him something of a smart man.

But yet here he stood at his sister's house. What he expected to prove by stopping at Martha's he didn't know. But if there was one person in his family who would not follow his father's every whim and wish to the exact letter, that person was Martha Byler Glick.

His boots were caked with mud by the time he walked from one side of his family's property to the other. Acres separated where David had moved to from where his sister now lived with Joshua in a house that he had heard through the grapevine his father had built for the two of them as a wedding present.

Most people would think that it was generous, but Samuel didn't feel that way. His father had only been generous when it had suited his purpose and his purpose in this was to keep Martha as close to him as possible. Of all the Byler children, Samuel was the most willful. Shortly after that was Martha.

Growing up, she hadn't caused as many problems as he had, but she did have a tendency to question everything. Questioning a lot of their beliefs and customs wasn't acceptable. Yet as long as she got an answer, she was fine. Still, she needed that answer. Samuel hadn't wanted an answer; he had just wanted to get away. A lot of good that had done him.

But if there was anybody who could tell him the state of affairs in the family, whether his *mamm*'s heart could be softened—whether he bent his knee or not—that person was Martha.

Coming home was harder than he had ever thought it would be. The truth of the matter was he never thought about coming back. He had made his life and he was going to live it. Then he saw the newspaper article, found out his brother had died and left a widow in need of care. He'd come home without a second thought and was now finding it more difficult than he'd ever imagined.

He had known that there would be those who would turn their backs on him for a great while, even after he got back right with the church. He just hadn't known he was going to have to battle his family quite so hard. Okay, so the truth was he had known in his heart, but he hadn't allowed himself to think about it. Now he stood at the edge of Martha's yard, half-hidden by two large oak trees planted there. They provided a bit of shade and a bit of camouflage from the road, and a bit of a hiding place for him to linger and watch his sister as she hung laundry on the line.

He had come here to talk to her, come here to find out how to make things right. Not just in the bending of his knee, but how to get his family to realize that he was truly sorry for everything that he had put them through. Unfortunately, they didn't know the half of it, but that was a good thing as well. His life had turned to more trouble even after his father had declared him dead.

He longed to hear Martha's voice again. Aside from his twin she was his favorite sibling. Yet there was a part of him that wanted to remain right where he was, hidden in the shade, watching from a distance, safe from the rejection that might come.

"You can come out now, Samuel Byler," Martha called to him. She didn't stop her chore, didn't turn to look at him or wave him over. She merely continued to hang up clothes in the cool fall air.

Samuel stepped out from behind the tree, a smile gracing his features. At least she was talking to him. "I didn't think you saw me."

She turned then and smiled at him and he could see that she was the same Martha that she had always been. Bright blue eyes and chocolate-brown hair, not as dark as what he and David boasted. "You were never any good at hide and seek."

"I just thought you were really good at finding me," he said.

She gave a small playful shrug. "That too, I suppose."

Samuel walked toward her slowly, stopping a good twenty feet from her. She was speaking to him, but that was all for now.

"I'm back," he said simply.

"Obviously," she said. "How long?"

"For good."

He said those two words, and she lost her

grip on a pair of Joshua's broadfall pants. They fell to the muddy ground. "Don't tease me like that, Samuel."

She snatched up the pants and tossed them over her shoulder. Then she turned back to the next article in the basket.

"I'm not teasing."

A small gasp escaped her, and she turned to face him fully. "Don't tease me with that either."

He shook his head. "I wouldn't dream of it." He was staying. He was staying for good. He was marrying David's widow. He was going to be a father to her three children. He had a lot of plans and they all revolved around him staying in Millers Creek. But he wasn't sure how much of any of those plans he should tell his sister.

"Does *Mamm* know?"

"She won't talk to me yet."

Martha nodded her firm chin. "You've got to get right with the church."

"Yeah," Samuel said. *"Jah,"* he corrected himself. "But even then, I'm not sure…" He allowed his words to trail off. He really didn't want to say them out loud. He really didn't want to admit that there was a chance that his mother might not ever speak to him, regardless of his standing. That she would continue to uphold Aaron Byler's wishes and claim that her son Samuel was dead. Knowing the words in his heart was bad enough, but to hear them spoken again was more than he thought he could handle.

"She will," Martha assured him.

How he wanted to believe that.

"You have to have faith," she said.

Faith. Now that was something he was running short on these days. But in truth, faith had nothing to do with why he was there. It had nothing to do with him recommitting his life to the church. It was all about a promise. That and nothing more.

Suddenly, Mattie's clear green eyes breezed through his thoughts. Why had he never noticed the sweetness in her gaze? Maybe because that sweetness died when she looked at him. Or maybe because back in the day, he had only been interested in leaving, not dating, or finding a wife or noticing that a girl's green eyes were the color of spring leaves after a rain. He pushed that thought away.

"Jah," he said again. "I suppose you're right."

Martha turned, and looked at him once more, her blue eyes studying him intently. He felt as if she could stare straight down to his soul. He might be older than her by a couple of years, but Martha had always had a wisdom that many others lacked. "Are you going to tell me the real reason why you came back?"

Her words took him aback. He managed to collect himself and shook his head. "I told you why I came back—"

She cut them off with a sad smile. "You and I both know that's not why you're here. Too many times I heard you say that once you got out of the valley, that you weren't ever coming back."

"Maybe I miss my family," he said.

"You know we get a lot of news from other parts of Pennsylvania here, right?"

He swallowed hard, trying to get the lump out of his throat. "Yeah."

"Just making sure." What she was really trying to say was that he didn't fool her one bit. That he could keep at it until the cows came home about reconciling with his family, but Martha knew there was another reason. Yet it was a reason he couldn't tell her. Not yet. Things were still too up in the air with Mattie.

Though he *was* marrying her. He had made up his mind about that the minute he'd seen the newspaper article and he wasn't changing it now.

"I'm here for good," he told her. "I'm staying."

"You talk to the bishop?"

"I'm planning on it."

She studied him once more, that gaze digging into him as if trying to root out all of his secrets. *"Jah,"* she finally said. She didn't believe him.

"I am." He hated that he felt he had to defend himself, but there it was. "Soon." It wasn't something that he was looking forward to. There were so many steps, so many vows and promises and so many weeks that would have to pass before he would be allowed back in. Before he would be allowed to marry Mattie. And yet he still had so many questions that no one could answer. They would all say faith, God's plan and all the like, and some of it, he was finding harder and harder to accept, even as time went by. But he had to pretend that it was what he wanted, even if in his heart he knew different.

"It's time," Martha said simply.

He knew that was true as well, but he had no words to reply.

Martha stooped down and picked up her laundry basket then turned to face him. "And the sooner the better."

He could only nod.

"Okay, now be gone with you, Samuel Byler. I'm expecting Joshua to come home for lunch, and I don't know what he would say if he found you here."

Mattie spent the rest of the afternoon cleaning through the ruined barrel of goat food and trying to salvage what she could from the practically new container. Thankfully the rain hadn't soaked all the way down and she was able to reclaim some from the bottom. She put that food in a plastic tub to help keep it dry and was standing with one hand pressed against her aching back and her eyes trained on the barn rafters, trying to decide just how she was going to get the leak repaired when Naomi came out looking for her.

"In here," she returned after Naomi called her name from outside the barn.

"What are you doing?" her sister asked as she stepped inside. "Lunch is almost ready and the girls are asking about you."

Because this time of day she was usually inside playing with them, cleaning, reading and otherwise resting. But not today. Today she was restless. Whether it was the weather, or the ruined food or the fact that Samuel's smile was starting to get to her. Every time he was near, she had to focus on that scar and remind herself that he wasn't David.

Well, that was what she told herself. Truthfully, they were so different in many, many ways that she was beginning to view him hardly as David's brother at all. Still she couldn't reconcile him with the angry young man who took off and caused his parents and family such grief.

There was something of that rebel in there, lingering around the lines bracketing his eyes and the downward turn of his mouth when he thought no one was looking. But he was trying. She could see that. What she didn't know was why.

"Do you think he honestly means to rejoin the church?" She hoped so, not so they could get married, but because it was hard to see someone lose their faith. Though at times she had wondered if he ever had any faith at all. Was his rebellion about finding out who he was, or had he turned away from God as well? And why did she care?

Naomi frowned at her. "What are you talking about?"

"Samuel," she replied.

"I know, Samuel. But why are you talking about him?"

"I don't know." Mattie shook her head. "Never mind."

Naomi studied her for a minute. "Come on in the house. We can talk about it over a cup of hot tea."

"That sounds wonderful." And it did. She needed to rest her back, get off her feet for a bit. Eat. Maybe everything wouldn't seem so confusing after lunch.

Naomi linked her arm with Mattie's and led her from the barn. They had only taken two steps toward the porch when Samuel appeared, walking up the lane that led to her house, a sack in one hand. He still wore David's coat. And for a moment she allowed herself the fantasy that it was David coming toward them and not his brother.

"And he's back," she muttered when she got her thoughts back on the right track.

"What's he want now?"

"I thought you were all for it," Mattie said. She didn't have to explain that she was talking about Samuel's marriage proposal.

Naomi shook her head. "He needs to be talking to the bishop, not…whatever it is he's doing now."

They stopped in the muddy yard, waiting for him to get near enough to speak and reveal his intentions.

He held up the brown paper sack. "I stopped by the hardware store and got some metal roof sealant. I need to fix that leak before it gets any worse."

"*I* need to fix it," Mattie countered. Yet she didn't know if she had the metal roof sealant on hand or not. That had been David's responsibility.

And now it's yours.

"No, you need to find someone to fix it for you, and here I am."

Mattie bit back a smart reply. Her father could

come and fix the leak, but she hated to ask him. He had his own troubles. Plus, he wasn't getting any younger. He didn't need to be climbing on roofs any more than absolutely necessary, and she couldn't say that her problem made it absolutely necessary for his attention.

"What about the *B*—" Mattie's words broke off as Naomi stepped on her foot. Good thing they were both wearing their muck boots. "Ow."

"Sorry," Naomi said."

Mattie frowned at her sister but said nothing.

"*Danki* for repairing that for us," Naomi continued, adding herself to the equation. That way the work he was doing wasn't just for Mattie; it was for them all. How could she complain about him fixing the roof for her family? She was a slick one that Naomi.

Her sister reached up and fiddled with her prayer *kapp*. For one time in her life, Mattie thought it was actually straight before she started messing with it.

"You're very welcome." His words sounded sincere. Okay, she knew they were sincere, but was it only because of a promise? How long before his need to help her wore off?

"Come on, Mattie." Naomi tugged on her arm and directed her away from the barn, away from Samuel. "We'll bring you out a sandwich when lunch is ready," Naomi called over one shoulder.

We will?

"I take it you haven't had lunch yet?" Naomi pressed.

Samuel shook his head. "But that's not necessary and the *Bann*—"

"Never mind all that. We'll bring out a sandwich and set it on a hay bale. Who are we to question if you happen to come up and eat it after we go back into the house?"

They were the people who would get called before the church for not adhering to a shunning, that's who!

Mattie managed to keep those words to herself as they made their way into the house. But she turned on her sister the minute they set foot inside and the door closed behind them. No, she turned *toward* her.

"*We'll* bring you a sandwich?" She tried to keep her tone level and calm, but she felt as if her words came out more like a screech.

"The man has to eat." Naomi shrugged.

"Not by my hand," Mattie countered.

"*Mamm.*" Bethann slid down from her seat at the table and came over to hug her around the legs.

Mattie's anxiety over feeding Samuel when he was under the *Bann* had to be pushed to the background. "Hello, *liebschdi.*" Mattie leaned down and kissed the top of her eldest's head, inhaling the sweet smell of her tropical-scented shampoo.

Gracie dragged one finger through her applesauce and happily licked it off.

Evie shook her head at her niece and handed the child another spoon. Maybe this time she would actually use it.

"Go back and finish your lunch. It's almost nap time."

"Jah, Mamm." Bethann did as Mattie bade.

"Tell her, Evie," Naomi jumped in.

"Tell her what?" Evie walked over, her crutches clanking with each step.

"Tell her that there's nothing wrong with Samuel fixing the leak in the barn roof and us feeding him lunch."

"I can't say that. He's under the *Bann*."

Mattie shot her sister a smug smile.

"But I will say that it's better to ask for forgiveness than to beg for permission." Evie grinned cheekily.

"Sister!" Mattie exclaimed.

Evie just shrugged as it was Naomi's turn to smile with smugness.

"I give it three days before the bishop is knocking on my door wanting an answer for my actions and all the two of you can do is stand there and grin like it's a good thing."

"I think Samuel coming back is a good thing," Evie said.

"That's not what I meant. It's a good thing for him to be back so he can bend his knee, ask for forgiveness and get himself back right with the church. It's a bad thing that he is hanging out here while he bides his time."

What was he waiting for? She didn't know. She supposed he had to do things in his own way, but with all his declarations to marry her, a body would think that he would be beating down the bishop's door trying to get it all back in place so they could get married.

He's not really serious.

The thought occurred to her so quickly it almost took her feet out from under her. Or maybe that was just Charlie who grabbed that opportunity to catch her from behind, pushing her nose into the bend of Mattie's knee. She buckled, but thankfully Naomi was there to catch her hand and steady her.

"Easy," Naomi said. "It's time for you to rest." She tried to lead Mattie to the table.

"I'm fine," Mattie protested, pulling her hand away, but continuing to the dining area to sit and eat. She was hungry, more so than normal. She supposed the combination of worry and pregnancy could do that to a woman.

"Something's bothering you," Naomi pressed.

Mattie eased down at the table next to her oldest and shook her head. "It's nothing. Just that if Samuel went by the hardware store on the way here…"

Did she really need to finish? She didn't know what he did each night or what he did in the time that he wasn't on her farm, but going by the hardware store was a surefire way to have the bishop come down on his head.

"Uh-oh." Evie muttered the sound, then clattered over to the window to look out.

"Please tell me he hasn't already fallen off the roof."

"Worse," she said, turning to face them. "The bishop's here."

"Samuel Byler!"

Samuel stopped smoothing the sealant over the seam in the roof that he had determined to be the cause of the leak and wiped one hand across his brow. The day had started off cool, but the sun was shining and he was working up a sweat crawling around on the top of the barn. He pushed to his feet and carefully made his way to the edge of the roof. *"Jah?"*

"Come down here. We need to talk to you."

Leroy Peachey had been the bishop of the Millers Creek district since as long as Samuel could remember, and when he had taken up his duties was not something people talked about. He was the bishop now, God's chosen to run the church, and that was all anyone needed to note.

Another man stood there next to Leroy, a man that Samuel didn't recognize. He decided as he gathered up his tools and supplies and made his way back down the ladder that the stranger must have recently moved to Millers Creek. At least in the time that Samuel had been gone. Eight years.

"Samuel, you remember Christ Peight."

Eight years, it turned out, was even longer than he realized. Christ Peight was his uncle by marriage. He had moved to the district a few years before Samuel left and had married Samuel's aunt Imogene. Imogene was his father's sister. How had he forgotten all that?

"Jah." He nodded and played off his momentary lapse of memory.

"Christ is our deacon now."

He hadn't been when Samuel left. Just another testament to the fact that things changed.

"You coming down now?" Leroy pressed.

Well, he hadn't really planned on it. That was why he had stayed exactly where he was when he heard the buggy rattling down the lane. Because once he came down, he knew what would happen next. His time for hiding out was over. It was time to fish or cut bait.

"Jah." He hated the reluctance he heard in his tone. But he supposed it would just be that way. How many people had he grown up with had faked their compliance with the church until true faith came to them? A handful at least. Being Amish wasn't easy, and that had nothing to do with lack of modern amenities and everything to do with heightened faith. Most had it. All were expected to. And when a crisis came, a line was drawn in the sand. Most stayed on the faithful side, but there were those who crossed over. Once a person did that, it was so very difficult to step back.

Samuel moved down from the ladder and made his way to where the men were standing next to their buggy. He shook hands with them and waited for them to say what was on their minds. He knew what it was; he knew what they were there for. He had known it would only be a matter of days before they found him, especially after his impromptu stop at the hardware store. But he couldn't let Mattie's roof go another week without fixing it. Or maybe deep down he wanted to get caught and that was why he had gone to the store to begin with. If it hadn't been for her leaky roof, it would have been something else.

He pushed that thought away and looked from one of them to the other, patiently waiting for them to continue. He wasn't going to make this easy for them.

"I believe you know why we're here," the bishop started.

Samuel momentarily toyed with the idea of asking them if they had come to help with Mattie's roof, but decided disrespect wouldn't gain him any ground in his community. Those words would be meant more as a joke than outright insult, but he was pretty sure they would be taken as such. The fire was lit. No sense throwing gasoline on it. "I believe so, *jah*."

Christ took a step forward. "We're here to make sure that you fulfill the promises you set forth when you were baptized."

What could he say to that? Samuel merely nodded. "I see."

At least his uncle didn't tell him all the rumors and such that he had heard from western Pennsylvania. Some of his escapades had to have made it this far out in the Amish grapevine. People moved from one community to another. Adult children left for other opportunities and then letters were written and word got around. *Did you know that...*

"I fully intend to restate my vows and ask for forgiveness. I know I have done wrong in the eyes of God and the church."

Christ looked to Leroy, who nodded. It

seemed Samuel's vow was good enough for the bishop. Now he had to convince himself to believe it.

"Worship is at your family's house tomorrow."

He already knew that. But tomorrow…that was too soon. He couldn't get his mind wrapped around all the consequences of forgiveness and all the sins he would have to confess. He couldn't confess them in front of everyone without first talking to Mattie. There were a few things she would have to know about him before he could hope he would ever be suitable to be her husband.

He heard the door to the house open, but he didn't turn to see who had come out. It was Mattie, he could feel her presence the way he used to be able to feel Emma's, a strong pull like a magnet. He knew she was there without even having to turn his head.

"I'll be there." He almost choked on the lie. He could try, but he couldn't promise. He couldn't say for certain he could convince his heart to give the church another chance by eight o'clock tomorrow morning.

He could feel her gaze on him as he shook their hands. Then they nodded to Mattie and climbed back into the bright yellow carriage. Samuel kept his eyes trained on the back of that buggy until it turned at the road and he could no longer see it.

"I suppose that was bound to happen sooner or later."

He turned as she spoke, not really knowing her mood until he fully faced her. She seemed calm, but they both knew that if this continued, she would be on the bad side of the church right alongside him. *"Jah."*

Which further testified to the possibility that maybe he needed the pressure from the church to do what was right. Maybe he needed someone on his case so he could get his life back like it needed to be so he could fulfill his promise to his brother.

"Did you mean that?" she asked. "Are you going to be at church tomorrow?"

"Jah." He knew he *needed* to be there. He knew time was ticking and there was no time like the present and all the other sayings that people used to hurry themselves into what they needed to do. He gave her a smile of reassurance.

He would try. It was all he could truly promise and even then, he didn't hold out hope.

He hated lying to her now. Knew that it was better to tell the truth, but the truth would make her hold him at a distance, keep him an arm's length away and right now that was something he couldn't bear.

"Good." Her smile was so bright he couldn't help but return it. Yet he knew, come tomorrow afternoon, she wouldn't be smiling at him with such sweetness.

Chapter Eight

Mattie craned her neck to the side, doing her best to see around Ginny Schrock. The woman was taller than most of the men in their district, including her husband, Elmer. But Mattie wasn't trying to see around the men, just Ginny.

"Would you sit still?" Evie admonished in a whisper.

"Sorry," Mattie whispered in return.

"He's not here." Naomi's soft tone matched theirs, but held a more exasperated note.

While the bishop and deacon had been talking to Samuel the day before, Mattie and her sisters had stood near the windows and watched. They couldn't hear what was going on, but according to the men's body language everything seemed to be okay and they certainly weren't shouting. Of course, Mattie didn't have personal experience of what would happen if the bishop

came out to talk about a person asking for forgiveness and getting oneself back right with the
church. It wasn't a conversation most Amish
ever had. Finally, she had given up guessing
and headed outside to see what was really happening.

She had heard it straight from the man himself. She had even asked him outright, and he
had promised her that he was coming to church
today to start the process of getting back in and
right and forgiven and all the other aspects of
ending a shunning. It wasn't an immediate act.
A person didn't leave and live a life away from
the church without having to show intent and
honesty in their renewed vows. It would be
a good six weeks or so before Samuel would
be fully welcomed back in. But now...that six
weeks would drag into eight, maybe longer if
he pulled this stunt again. The bishop could be
a hard man when it came to leaving the faith.

One thing was certain: the quicker he confessed, the quicker he would be forgiven.

"He said he would be here," she whispered
to Naomi.

"Well, he's not," she said in return.

"He promised."

Naomi's mouth twisted into a frown and
Mattie knew exactly what it meant. Her sister
was afraid that Mattie wouldn't marry Samuel,

couldn't marry Samuel if he didn't get right with the church once more. But this wasn't about that.

He was her brother-in-law—she had known him most of her life. Of course she wanted him to get his life right, to protect his soul. It had nothing to do with his marriage proposal.

She looked across the way to where her father sat, each of her girls on either side of him. They missed their *dat*, and they needed a man in their lives. So she needed Samuel to be in her girls' lives. At first, she had worried that it would confuse them, but as time went on and they grew older it would become clearer to them. And she could only hope from there that he would be a positive influence for them. But not if he wasn't around because he was shunned.

Evie clasped Mattie's hand in her own and squeezed her fingers reassuringly. "It'll be okay," she promised.

"I hope you're right."

Mattie and her sisters left early after the church service. That was the life of a dairy farmer. She might only have goats, but they needed to be milked at a certain time just like cows. Every day. Even Sunday.

They had actually stayed a bit longer than regular. The girls were having too good of a time sharing their crackers with peanut butter spread and cup cheese with their *dawdi*. Mattie was loath to break up their time together. It seemed since Samuel had arrived at her house, she'd had a harder time getting away to visit with her father. Consequently that meant her daughters hadn't been visiting much either.

They were almost home when Mattie turned to Evie, who was seated next to her. Naomi was in the back with the girls. "He wasn't there."

"You didn't see him," Evie corrected.

"He wasn't there."

"Okay," Evie agreed. "I didn't see him either. But that doesn't mean that he wasn't there. He could have been there and we just didn't see him."

"And afterward? Where was he during the meal?"

Evie gave a small shrug. "Maybe he had to leave and go attend something where he is staying. Do you even know where he is staying?"

Mattie shook her head. "But I heard him promise the bishop and the deacon that he would be there."

"And you don't know if there were any other conversations before that one that you didn't hear?"

"Why do you like him so much?"

Evie frowned. "It's not a matter of like. It's

more…" She paused as if searching for the right words. "There's something in his eyes, a pain or a hardship, something that has caused him such grief. And I think that he needs you to help him over that as much as you need him."

"Why would you say that?" Mattie asked.

"Because I see the same thing in your eyes."

What was a woman to say to that?

Mattie was silent for the rest of the trip home as she contemplated her sister's observations. Were they even real or something from those contraband romance novels that Evie liked to read when she thought no one was looking?

Mattie hadn't seen anything akin to pain in his eyes. The only thing that she noted was the faraway tone his voice took when speaking about God, as if religion and the Lord were unattainable. And if he believed that…

She pushed those thoughts aside as she pulled to a stop next to the house. A familiar sound met her ears. It was coming from the milking barn.

"Is that what I think it is?" Evie asked.

"I'm afraid it might be," Naomi returned.

Mattie didn't say anything. She couldn't. She was too busy trying to plan her next move—aside from marching into the milking parlor and giving Samuel the what for. She had her girls to think about, the horse, putting the carriage away and a host of other things that had to be done.

Except not the milking, because it seemed that he had started that without her.

She supposed it was Samuel. Who else would come onto her property and milk the goats?

"Go on," Evie said. "I've got the girls."

Naomi nodded. "I'll take care of the horse and such."

Mattie shot her sisters a tight smile. *"Danki."* And she managed to hold in her temper as she made her way into the milking barn.

As she had suspected, Samuel was inside, the goats on the raised platform munching away at the organic hay mixture she bought for this very purpose, milking machines pumping away.

"You're home." He smiled at her and her heart melted just a bit at the sweet gesture. But she couldn't let him get away with this.

"You," she started, resisting the urge to point an accusing finger at him. "You were supposed to be at church today."

At least he had the decency to look ashamed of himself. "About that—"

"You promised." She couldn't stop the ring of distrust that crept into her voice. She didn't want him to know how badly he had hurt her. How she had been looking forward to today.

"I didn't promise."

"You—"

"I didn't promise," he said again, his tone so

quiet and solemn that she could barely hear it above the machines.

She thought back to the conversation they had had the day before. Okay, so he hadn't promised. She had wanted to hear that and so she had believed it.

"Maybe you didn't say the words, but now you are just splitting hairs."

It was the truth and he knew it. At least he had the decency to duck his head.

"I'm not ready," he finally admitted.

"Not ready." She repeated the words and even to her own ears they sounded somewhere between a statement and a question.

"It's complicated," he said.

"When is it not?"

He looked up at her then, his expression unreadable. "There's something I need to talk to you about," he started. But he broke off as Naomi stuck her head inside the milking barn.

"Is Charlie in here?" she asked.

Mattie shook her head. "What would she be doing in here?" Then she turned to Samuel. "You didn't get her out of the house, did you?"

"No," he replied.

"Evie just came out onto the porch. She can't find Charlie anywhere."

"She probably got shut up in the playroom again." The mischievous goat was forever going into the girls' playroom upstairs and falling asleep under a blanket or the crib, in the closet or the toy box and then not waking up until everyone was gone and the door was closed. It had happened too many times to count.

Naomi shook her head.

"Did you check under my bed?"

"I didn't. I was putting the horse away, but Evie said she checked everywhere."

Mattie trusted her sister, but who was to say that she had truly checked *everywhere*. "Have you seen her since we got back?"

"No. And I don't think Evie has either."

A pang of dread shot through Mattie. Charlie could have gotten out when they got home or before they left for church...hours ago. And if that were the case she could be practically anywhere in the valley.

She turned back to Samuel.

He waved a hand in the general direction of the barn door. "Go see about it," he told her. "I've got this."

She didn't even have to say the words. She didn't have to remind him how important the goat was to her girls. He just knew and for that she was grateful.

Mattie shot him a thankful smile, then started toward the house.

"Mattie," Evie urgently greeted her as she

walked inside. She already had both girls seated at the table enjoying a snack. It would probably ruin their dinners, but at least they were occupied. "I'm sorry. I don't know where she is."

"She has to be around here somewhere." Mattie hoped that she was. But Mattie wasn't laying that on her sister. It wasn't Evie's fault.

The front door opened, and Naomi dashed inside. "Did you find her?" she asked on a rush.

"Not yet."

"I've come to help. The horse is put away—I can do the buggy after we find Charlie."

Mattie gave a quick nod of thanks to her sister and they began to work.

They started at the attic and searched from the top of the house to the bottom. Midway, Samuel came in and joined them. No one reminded him that this was a special case, that he shouldn't be in the house with them. They just kept searching.

With each floor they covered, Mattie's heart sank a little more. What if Charlie had gotten out of the house and no one noticed? She was forever darting outside, around people, between their legs, always causing mischief. But if she had gotten loose and was hurt or bleeding? Or dead...

She couldn't allow herself to think that.

"You don't think she could have gotten into

the basement?" Evie looked horrified at the thought. It was almost as bad as Mattie's own thoughts about the pygmy getting outside.

"It'll be all right," Naomi said. "As long as the tomato fence held up." Her sister was just trying to be diplomatic. The "tomato fence" was more of a dividing wall of chicken wire and two-by-fours that David had built when Evie started growing tomatoes inside. The only way for the goat to get inside would be for it to have been left open. That meant a mistake on Evie's part when she went down to check on the tomatoes last.

"Tomato fence?" Samuel asked. He hadn't spoken since he'd joined their search.

"Come on." Mattie motioned for him to follow her down the stairs toward the basement door.

Up above, she noted to herself, Evie stopped to give the girls something more to keep them occupied while they finished searching the house. More cookies to ruin their supper, no doubt. But that was what good *aentis* were for, she supposed.

The door leading to the basement was closed, and with a normal pet that should seem to indicate that they weren't inside. However, Mattie knew, with Charlie anything was possible. She stopped on the stairs, unable to open the door.

"What's wrong?" Samuel asked. He was directly behind her, one step up from where she stood. Naomi and Evie were directly behind him

"If she got in with the tomatoes…" She didn't finish the sentence. She couldn't bring those words out into the open. They were bad enough in her mind.

"What?" Samuel asked.

"Tomato plants," Evie started. "The leaves and stems are poisonous to goats. As are the unripened fruit. That's why David built the fence."

"Would she eat the plants?" Samuel asked. "Don't they taste bad? Wouldn't she know they aren't good for her?"

"She's a goat," Naomi said simply.

He nodded once. "Right. Goat." Then he turned back toward the door and nudged Mattie to one side. "I'll go."

"You will?" She couldn't keep the relief from her voice. She had been standing there just wondering what she was going to say to her girls, especially Bethann, about where Charlie had gone. Would it be enough to just say the goat was now in heaven with her *dat*? Would Bethann begin to ask why heaven got to have all the things that she loved?

"Of course."

"*Danki*, Samuel, I—"

"No thanks needed." He reached around her so very close as he opened the door.

She pressed her back to the side of the stairwell so he could move past her and inside the room. Then Mattie held her breath as she waited for his report.

"Nothing," he called the moment before he reappeared in the doorway. "She's not down here."

"Are you sure?" Mattie asked, hoping against hope. If she wasn't in the basement…

"She must have gotten outside."

The relief of not finding Charlie poisoned in the basement was short-lived. How long had she been out?

"Let's go," Naomi called as they all turned around to go back up the stairs. But with Evie in the lead it was slow going.

"I'm going as fast as I can."

Mattie tamped down her impatience with the time it was taking Evie to navigate the stairs, reminding herself that it was amazing that Evie could even manage the stairs at all. And patience was a virtue. But finding the goat…

Finally, they all filed back into the kitchen, a feat that seemed to take a lifetime.

"What about outside?" Samuel asked.

Mattie nodded.

"Mamm!" Gracie called, slapping her hands against the high chair tray. *"Mamm."*

"Hello, sweetie." Mattie bent to kiss the top of her head, needing the familiar touch. Where was her goat?

"I'll stay with the girls," Evie said. "I'm not that fast anyway."

Mattie smiled her thanks. "You're the best," she told her younger sister.

Evie dimpled in return, but Mattie could see the worry in her eyes. "That's what they tell me."

Naomi, Samuel and Mattie filed onto the porch and started their search of the yard, the barn and the rest of the outbuildings, including the playhouse David had built for Bethann's first birthday.

But Charlie was nowhere to be found. They called her name and searched and searched again until Mattie was certain they had looked in every nook and cranny the farm had. Still no Charlie.

They had gathered back again, in front of the steps that led to the porch. Evie had stepped out with the girls, shading her eyes with one hand. "No?" she asked none of them in particular.

It was Samuel who answered. "It's like she disappeared."

"Goats don't disappear," Naomi said dryly while Mattie silently reiterated the sentiment. She couldn't have disappeared. She was a goat.

A solid creature. She had to be around somewhere.

"Up." Gracie raised one hand in the air, signifying that she wanted to be held.

"I can't carry you, *liebschdi*," Evie replied.

"I'll get her." Mattie stepped forward, but stopped when Samuel laid a hand on her arm.

"Let me," he said.

Part of her wanted to refuse. Was she just confusing her girls by allowing him to hang around? And what of his promise to rededicate his life to the church? But she was too tired and worried to argue. She nodded her consent and watched as he stepped forward and scooped her daughter into his arms.

Gracie smiled and patted her hands on either side of his face, but at least she didn't break Mattie's heart by calling him *Dat*. "Up." Once more she raised one hand in the air.

"Is this not high enough?" He turned to look back at Mattie.

She could only shrug as his eyes questioned hers. What did her daughter want?

"Well, I'll be," he said, smiling as he shook his head.

"What?" Mattie asked.

He gestured up and to some spot behind her. "See for yourself."

Mattie turned and it took a moment for her to

train her gaze in the right spot. It was Charlie, curled up on top of the carriage, watching them as if this all was merely a marvelous game that she had just won.

Chapter Nine

"That goat," Evie muttered sometime later. After they had managed to get the goat down from the top of the carriage, with Samuel's help of course. After Samuel had gone back to wherever it was that he was staying and they had eaten their small supper, after the girls had been bathed and read to and finally put to bed, now the sisters were sitting in the living room recounting the scary events of the afternoon.

"Did you know a goat would do that?" Naomi asked.

Mattie shrugged. "I've heard stories, but I've never seen anything like that with my own eyes."

Evie shook her head once more. "That goat." *Jah.* That about summed it all up.

"Maybe we should get one of those gates to go on the porch steps. You know, to keep her from being able to get out into the yard." Naomi looked at each of them in turn to see what they thought of her idea.

Mattie shook her head. "I don't think the bishop would go for that at all."

Leroy Peachey was quite particular about the look of their houses. He wouldn't want anyone to mistake a yellow-topper's dwelling for one belonging to a more liberal black-topper. And with all the trouble she had stirred up already having her husband's shunned brother hanging around, she didn't need to add any more sins to her side of the scorecard.

"*Jah*, you're probably right," Naomi said.

"Where do you suppose he's staying?" Evie asked.

Naomi frowned. "The bishop?"

"No." Evie scoffed. "Samuel."

"That was my question too." Mattie tried to play it off, but she knew exactly who Evie was talking about.

"I don't know," Naomi said. "Mattie?"

"I don't know either." But it was something that she had often wondered herself. He couldn't be staying with anyone in the valley. At least no one Amish. Maybe he had made an *Englisch* friend or two, but as far as she remembered from what David had told her, Samuel had moved to the western part of the state just after leaving Millers Creek. He never said as much, but it seemed like *just after* didn't leave a great deal of time for making friends across religious divides.

"You don't think his sister..." Naomi started.

Mattie shook her head. She had seen Martha Glick at church that very morning. "If he was staying with Martha, she would have made him come to church today."

"You think?" Evie said.

"Positive," Mattie claimed. "Besides, I don't think Joshua would allow him to stay with them and not be right with the church."

"I agree with that. Joshua can be a—"

"Naomi." Mattie lowered her voice in sisterly warning.

"What?" Naomi asked, eyes wide with a feigned innocence. "I was going to say *stickler.*"

Perhaps the nicest description any of them had for Joshua Glick. None of them could see what a sweet person like Martha saw in such a man. Such was love, as they say.

"Maybe you should ask him," Evie said.

"Ask who?" Somehow Mattie had lost the thread of the original conversation.

"Ask Samuel where he's staying," Evie explained.

"What difference will that make?" Naomi asked.

"I don't know. But what if he's staying someplace horrible, like a run-down inn or a questionable B and B?"

"Questionable how?" Naomi demanded.

"What kind of inn?" Mattie asked.

"Oh, go on, both of you," Evie returned. "There's something up though. I can sense it."

It was true that Evie somehow had a sense about other people. Everyone except Freeman Yoder, it seemed, but now was not the time to bring that up.

"I'll ask him if I see him again," Mattie promised.

"Does that mean he won't be here first thing in the morning for the a.m. milking?" Evie pressed.

"No," she said wearily. "He'll be here."

It was a wonder that he heard her clear her throat over the noise of all the milking machines, or perhaps not. He had been wondering when she would make it out to the barn.

"Samuel," she said, coming up next to him.

"Mattie."

"What time did you get here?" she asked.

"Just a bit ago." Long enough before now he had already brought in the first few goats, cleaned them, hooked them to the milking machines and was just about to finish up with this round when she stepped inside.

"You can't keep doing this," she told him.

He didn't acknowledge her words, just started unhooking the beasts one by one and directing them back out into the pasture. He had been here on Mattie's farm enough to know that they wouldn't stay there for long. Not when the weather was as cool as it was when they had woken up that morning.

A thin coating of frost covered everything from the tops of the grass to the tops of the buildings. Winter was definitely on its way. He had long since learned that goats preferred the warm comforts of the shelved barn his brother built to any outdoor activities when it was this cold.

Most dogs seemed to like scampering around in the cool air. Horses didn't seem to mind all that much, nor did cows, but goats, it seemed, were definitely their own.

"I don't know why not," he finally said.

"The bishop—"

"Will probably be back out today or tomorrow and I'll promise to go back to church the next service."

"But will you do it this time?" Her words rang between them.

It was quiet in the milking parlor. The goats

that had been milked were already out and the next round weren't inside yet.

He turned toward her and smiled. "Of course."

She studied him until he finally turned away under the guise of letting in more goats. The truth was he couldn't take her scrutiny much longer.

Thankfully, she didn't ask him any more questions, just grabbed a rag and a bucket of disinfectant and started to work. Together they completed the task in silence, neither one needing to say anything to the other. The act of being together, working together, was somehow so intimate, more than he would've ever dreamed.

Jah, he had to get himself right with the church. No more delays. He owed Mattie and David that.

"Samuel," she said once the last goat had been released back into the pasture and the milking stalls had all been wiped down and readied for the afternoon milking. "Where are you staying?"

"I…" He didn't know what to tell her. He certainly didn't want to tell her that he'd camped on her land without permission.

He looked at her then deep into those apple-green eyes. He had to tell her the truth.

"I pitched a tent at the edge of the property."

She seemed to choke on her reply. "At the edge... At the edge of my property?"

"Or AJ's property, I suppose." His brother lived on the adjacent farm from where David and Mattie had set up house. "Depends on which direction you're facing, I guess."

She closed her eyes and shook her head just slightly. He might not have even noticed if it had not been for the wiggle of her prayer *kapp* strings. Then she opened her eyes once more. "You've been staying in a tent."

"Yes. I didn't think anyone would take me in and—" He ended on a shrug. "I had some troubles before I came out here, and I don't really have a lot of money. Not that I'm complaining," he backpedaled. "Just that I couldn't stay in a hotel or anything and I wanted to be close so I can help you."

"It snowed." Her voice was incredulous, waiting for him to tell her something different.

"Yes. And it was cold. But it wasn't the end of the world. Like I said, I didn't want anyone to go against the bishop and let me stay with them."

"Your *mamm*?" she asked.

"Wouldn't even let me on the porch," he admitted. If he had explained, maybe had a chance to talk to her even just a bit, he might've been able to soften her stance, but he didn't want a welcome out of guilt. He wanted a welcome because he was family and they knew what truly was in his heart. A person couldn't get that just walking up out of the blue after eight years. That much he knew for a fact.

"I have a feeling I'm going to regret this," she said on a sigh. "You can stay here in the barn. Go get your things. Tent, sleeping bag, whatever you have. You can't be out in the elements. We're supposed to have another cold front come in."

He shook his head. "I've been through worse." And he had. He wasn't bragging; it was simply the truth.

"Samuel, there was frost on everything this morning. It's November."

What were a couple of days out in the cold compared to losing Emma? Compared to Mattie losing David? But he was here now and he was going to make everything right.

"Danki."

"Please don't make me regret this." Her tone was so urgent, so heartfelt he wanted to do something to ease away that anxiety.

"What would I do that would make you regret it?" Did she think so little of him?

"I don't know, Samuel. Things are never as they seem these days."

He couldn't fault her with that one. He wasn't quite what he seemed either, but he would tell her soon. He would have to tell her before he went before the church. She deserved to know. But not now. Not yet.

"I meant what I said, Mattie. About the church. Next service I'll be there."

She studied his face, and he knew she was looking for any indication that he was sincere. And he was. He would go before the church, and it would be the next church service. It had to be the next church service. He couldn't go on staying in her barn or in a tent; he couldn't go on not having any contact with his family. And he couldn't go on without knowing he had done everything he could and followed the steps he needed to follow in order to marry her. Somehow now it seemed more urgent than it did when he arrived. He wanted to get to know those two little girls better. He wanted to get to know Mattie better. He may have known her once upon a time so many years ago. But he was different now, and she surely was as well. He wanted to show her that he meant what he said, not just about joining the church but about marrying her and making her family complete once more.

"You don't have to convince me," she said. She reached up and touched the side of his face, then she drew her hand back as if his skin were fire. "It's the bishop you'll need to prove it to. And I'm sure he'll be here this afternoon to find out exactly why you weren't at church today." And with that still ringing in his ears, she turned and left the milking barn.

"You did what?" Naomi's question was more of a screech.

"What happened to 'you should marry him'? If we get married, he'll do more than stay in the barn," Mattie shot back. She and Naomi had been working a puzzle at the dining table when Mattie had decided to tell her sister about the invitation she had given Samuel. To stay in the barn until he could find a place to live.

Regardless of her sisters' suggestions otherwise, she wasn't going to marry him. He was too much like David. And too different from David. It was all so very confusing. Just touching him so briefly made her feel like she was touching a wet battery, a zing shooting straight through her. It put her on the edge, made her anxious. It made her want to run away and at the same time lean in close. And frankly, right now she wasn't up for either.

"I was talking about once he gets himself back right with the church. If he gets back right with the church, invite him to stay in the guest room. What do I care other than I would have to sleep on the couch?" Naomi asked. "And yet you invite him, he who is shunned, to sleep in your barn. What do you think the bishop is going to say about that?"

"Nothing, because he's not going to know. I'm not gonna tell him, you're not gonna tell him, Samuel's not going to tell him."

"And you don't think he's going to find out on his own?"

"Who's going to find out what?" Evie asked, picking that time to come through the house. She looked from one of her sisters to the other, her blue eyes questioning. She had their father's eyes. In fact, she was Thomas Ebersol straight over again.

Naomi braced her hands on the table in front of her and turned to Evie. "Mattie has invited Samuel to stay in the barn."

Evie seemed to think about it a second, then she eased herself down across from Mattie and next to Naomi. Somehow, to Mattie, it seemed like the two of them against her. Or maybe she just was feeling defensive since Naomi obviously did not agree with her decision.

"And you're afraid that the bishop is going to find out?" Her question was more directed at Mattie than Naomi.

Mattie sat back in her chair, one hand fluttering to her chest. "I'm not afraid that the bishop's going to find out, because I don't think the bishop is going to find out. Your sister thinks that he might and feels like I will be in some sort of trouble if he does."

"I don't think—I know. Samuel Byler staying in your barn will get back to the bishop and then there will be trouble."

"He's promised to get things right at the next church service. I don't think even the bishop would agree with him staying in a tent at the edge of the property in the middle of November just to satisfy the remains of a shunning."

Evie shook her head. "I don't know. Leroy can be something of a stickler when he wants to be."

"Christ is Samuel's uncle. And the deacon. You don't think he can put in a word for his nephew?"

"Maybe," Evie said. "What concerns me most is this promise. Did he promise last time? Just yesterday?"

Mattie closed her eyes and shook her head. "I may have mistaken his words as a promise. Thinking back, I knew he was never going to go to this church service. But he'll be at the next one."

"How can you be so certain?" Naomi said.

"Again, I thought you were all for the two of us getting married. Now you don't even want him staying in the barn nor do you believe that he's ready to bend his knee and ask for forgiveness."

"I wasn't going to bring this up," Naomi started. She picked at a spot on the table. Most likely jelly that had been missed in today's cleaning. "But when I was in town today, I heard talk."

"There's always talk," Mattie countered. But her heart started to beat a tad faster.

"What are they saying?" Evie asked.

"I'm not going to repeat it," Naomi said. "Who knows if even any of it is true?"

But most rumors started with some sort of truth and they all knew it.

"I just think you and Samuel need to have a really big talk before he moves into the barn."

Mattie shook her head. "If I can't trust David's brother, who can I trust?"

"It's not about trust," Naomi said. "Eight years can change a person. I'm just asking you to find out who he is now."

"He's a person, that's who he is. David's brother. A member of my family, just like the two of you, and I certainly wouldn't make either one of you sleep in a tent, shunned or not." Mattie stood. She grabbed her shawl off the hook by the door. She needed a breath. Some fresh air.

"*Mamm*, where you go?"

She turned and smiled at Bethann. She and

her sister were playing on the living room floor. Bethann was pretending to read books to Gracie and their dolls while Gracie pretended that she understood.

"Just outside for a minute."

"I go too."

Mattie shook her head. "You stay inside. I'll be back in a minute." But the delay was enough to cool her ire a bit. She sighed as she stepped out onto the porch. The need to rush off was gone, replaced by a sadness she couldn't understand. She had come to terms with David's death weeks ago. This was different.

She wrapped her shawl a little tighter around her shoulders and started down the steps. She allowed her feet to take her to the barn. All the while pretending that it wasn't a conscious decision to go there, to see if Samuel got settled in okay. To see if he needed anything.

He came out of the barn just as she was coming up, a bag slung over one shoulder.

"Are you going somewhere?" she asked.

He gave her an apologetic smile. "Yeah," he said almost sheepishly. "Back to my tent."

Mattie frowned. "I thought you were going to stay here for a while. In the barn."

"About that…" He shifted uncomfortably and she had the feeling he didn't want to tell her the rest. "I appreciate the offer and all, but I have a fire at my campsite."

"Okay. Do you need an extra blanket?"

He shook his head. "It's not for warmth— I use it to warm up my food. Canned goods. I can't really have a fire in your barn."

She felt like an idiot, but not so much so that she wanted to take back her invitation. Regardless of what Evie or even Naomi thought about Samuel, she was growing accustomed to having him around. That didn't mean she was going to marry him, but she wanted him near. She wanted her children to get to know their *onkel*. It might be confusing at first, but they would come to understand. "I'm sorry. I didn't think about food. Of course I will bring you something out to eat."

He shot her an indulgent smile. "Now, Mattie, you know the bishop is not going to like it if you continually give me food. Whether we sit at the same table or not."

She shook back her head in defiance. "I'll leave a plate of food out. Things just happen."

"Not like that, they don't, and we both know it."

Her heart fell. "So you're not going to stay in my barn?"

He shook his head. "I'm sorry. No." He

started past her, and she stood there dumbly and watched him walk away.

"But you're coming back tomorrow, right?" she called after him.

He turned around and shot her a charming smile that further increased her heart rate. "I'll be here."

Chapter Ten

Monday afternoon, the bishop showed just as expected. This time he brought all the members of the church leadership with him. They made a sight climbing out of the bright yellow buggy with their blue shirts and black pants and varying lengths of beards.

As the oldest of the four, Leroy Peachey's beard was the whitest and the longest. His impressive facial hair reached down past the fifth button on his shirt, while the other men had beards, all shorter in length and darker in color.

Mattie stood at the window and watched as they approached the barn. They seemed to know that they would find Samuel there and went straight to the point instead of sharing any niceties with her and her sisters. She knew it was only a matter of time before they knocked on her door to have a talk about the situation.

As she watched, the girls played behind her. Evie was at the table writing something to go into *The Budget*, the countrywide Amish newspaper, and Naomi had gone home for a bit. It was her turn to clean their *dawdi*'s *dawdihaus*, a sort of grandparent's apartment attached to the house where their father lived. She would be back before supper, but Mattie was certain that she would not be happy that she missed the excitement of the bishop come calling.

Of course it might be a good thing seeing as how he brought out the entire church leadership with him.

She couldn't hear what they were saying but knew what was being said. Basically, anyway. They were telling him that in order to be welcomed back into the community that he had to adhere to the laws of God and man and the church. He had to bend his knee and ask for forgiveness, then outline his sins for the congregation and have them vote on whether or not he would be allowed back in. Of course he would. That was one part of shunning that outsiders didn't understand. It wasn't about separation but bringing the person back into the fold.

Still, Samuel would then spend another six or so weeks, maybe even more, continuing to be under the *Bann*. He wouldn't be able to eat with them, they couldn't exchange money with him, and a host of other things. But once that time was over, he would be welcomed back with wide-open arms.

With a sigh, she moved away from the window and into the kitchen.

"What's the matter?" Evie asked.

"I'm going to make a pot of coffee. The bishop is here. And he'll want to talk to me next."

"I'm not leaving." Evie stood and practically defended her sister right there on the spot.

"You don't have to leave, but let me do the talking."

"There are cookies. The ones that the girls and I made the other day."

Mattie smiled with the memory. The making of them consisted mostly of eating cookie dough and feeding it to Charlie, but there were at least a dozen cookies complete when they were finished.

As if she knew that Mattie was thinking about her, the goat hopped off the couch and trotted over to where she stood. The beast butted her head against her leg almost like a cat would do. Mattie considered it a sign of affection. She bent down and scooped her up before making her way into the kitchen.

"You can't make coffee with a goat on your hip," Evie called behind her.

Mattie shook her head, still smiling. "There's where you're wrong. I'm a *mamm* and I can do almost anything with a kid on my hip."

Evie laughed at the pun and the good mood lasted clear up until the moment the bishop and other church elders knocked on her door.

"How did it go with the bishop this afternoon?"

Naomi had pulled Mattie aside the moment she and Evie arrived at their *vatter*'s house. It was family dinner night, a substitute for the upcoming Thanksgiving holiday. There was a wedding that day that their father was attending. It happened often during a wedding season, especially as communities grew larger. Mattie didn't mind. She was looking forward to a smaller gathering, just her and her girls and Evie. Naomi and her twin, Priscilla, as well as their other sisters, Lizzie and Sarah Ann, were all going with their *dat*.

Mattie didn't ask Evie why she wasn't attending, but she had a feeling it had something to do with Mattie not going either. She should, she knew, but she had begged off, stating the work she had to do and that she couldn't get anyone to help her this time of year. Her cousin seemed not to be too disappointed and for that Mattie was grateful. She didn't want to hurt her cousin's feelings, but she just wasn't up for a wedding.

She would have to get ready though; Evie was bound and determined to attend Freeman Yoder and Helen Schrock's wedding, and Mattie couldn't let her go to that alone. At least not without sisterly support. But she had till the end of the year to come to terms with that one.

Naomi pinched her arm.

"Ow," Mattie cried, jerking away from her sister. "What was that for?"

"You drifted. I wanted to get your attention back."

Mattie frowned at her. "You could have said my name."

Naomi shrugged. "This worked too."

Sisters.

"So…" Naomi prompted. "The bishop."

"I don't know what he said to Samuel. He had to leave before we could really talk. I'm sure the same talk that anyone would get if they'd strayed."

"And what did he say to you?"

It was Mattie's turn to shrug. "Same thing. Samuel isn't allowed in the house. You know how it goes. He did tell me that he would overlook Samuel helping me at the farm. It's good for him to serve time being part of the community again before he's actually back in."

"And Samuel is coming to the next church service to ask for forgiveness from the congregation?"

"That's my understanding."

"Do you believe him?"

Did she? "I want to. I know it can't be easy, but it's got to be done. It must be done."

"And then you will accept his proposal?"

Mattie opened her mouth to answer, but no words came out. She should have said a solid *nay*, but she didn't and thankfully she was spared having to answer as Priscilla joined them, one of her fourteen-month-old daughters on her hip.

"What are you two whispering about?"

"Where's the other?" Mattie asked.

"*Dat*'s got her." That was the problem with having twins and being a young widow. She only had two hands and no husband to help.

Priscilla bounced the toddler up and down. From the piece of ribbon tied around her wrist, Mattie knew that she held Leona. The girls were identical and so hard to tell apart that Priscilla had to have some way to let people know which one was which. A piece of ribbon did the trick. "So what are you whispering about?"

Naomi shot her sister a sassy look. "You."

Priscilla reached up with her free hand and smoothed Naomi's prayer *kapp* back into the proper place. "If you used more pins," she started.

"Jah, jah," Naomi scoffed. "I've heard it all before."

Sometimes Mattie thought Naomi might not completely pin her prayer covering into the proper place just to be different. But she had never outright asked her. It wasn't that Naomi and Priscilla looked all that much alike. They each favored a parent. Priscilla had brown hair and blue eyes like their father and Evie. While Naomi was blond like Mattie, but with eyes that couldn't decide if they wanted to be blue or green.

"Dinner," Sarah Ann called. She had a very content Gracie propped on one hip. It was the same every time they came over. Sarah Ann scooped up the child and carried her around constantly, kissing the top of her head intermittently. Bethann had gotten too independent of late and preferred to do everything herself.

Everyone gathered around the table and settled in. Just before their prayer, Mattie glanced around at all of her sisters, her father and her children gathered there with her. It was good to be together like this. These were the times when she missed her mother the most. Anna Grace Ebersol had died from cancer just after Mattie's eighteenth birthday. It had been a crushing time for her, even though they knew that her time was near. Yet at least she had memories to share, unlike Sarah Ann, the youngest, who had only been six and could barely remember any of their mother. Sarah Ann relied on the others to recount the happy tales of Anna Grace's wonderful life.

Only one person was missing this year that had been there the last and that was David. So why was it Samuel's face that appeared before her? Why did she feel like he should be there today?

Because he was alive and crouched down in the woods somewhere sleeping in a tent and warming canned food on a fire. It just didn't seem right. And she vowed to make him a plate and take it to him just as soon as they got home. Then she bowed her head and prayed for forgiveness.

"Samuel?" It had taken Mattie fifteen minutes at least to find Samuel's camp. She only knew that it was close to the edge of her property where it ran into the Byler's property but nothing more. So armed with a flashlight and her big coat, she made her way across the fields and into the woods nearby.

The tent rustled, and she could see a light moving around inside. Then suddenly there he was. "Mattie?" The surprise in his voice was evident. He hadn't expected her.

Come to think of it, she really hadn't expected to be here either. But once the idea took root in her mind, she couldn't let it go. *Jah*, it was all about forgiveness. But for him it was also about starting over. And starting over wasn't a punishment. The thought of him out here eating a can of beans or some kind of ready-made meal hurt her heart. David wouldn't want that for his brother. She didn't want that for his brother. She didn't want that for Samuel.

"I—I—" she stammered. "I brought you something to eat." He tilted his head to one side and studied her as much as he could, considering the shadows surrounding them. They both held flashlights, but the world around them was pitch-black. It was as if they were suspended there together with nothing else around but the stars.

"You brought me something to eat?"

"I just—" She couldn't tell him. She couldn't tell him that she had been at dinner and she felt bad for him. That she had been thinking about him the entire time. That she had worried about him. That she hated that he was sleeping in this tent and all the other parts of the shunning he was experiencing as he tried to come back into the community. That this and so much more were eating away at her. "We had leftovers at supper and I thought you might enjoy them." Not quite a lie. Not quite the truth either.

She went to hand the container to him and thought better of it. She set it down on the ground outside his tent. There wasn't a rule against handing food to someone, but she figured erring to caution was the best course of action.

"You didn't have to do that," he said.

She nodded, then felt dumb for doing so. "I wanted to." Another half-truth. She wanted to, but she needed to just as much.

"I— Thank you."

She fisted her free hand in her pocket. The one that held the flashlight was a little unsteady. She hoped he didn't notice. It was time to leave. She needed to go now. She hadn't thought about the isolation when she walked out here with the food. She hadn't thought about it nor had her sisters brought it up. She was surprised that neither Naomi nor Evie thought about it when she grabbed the flashlight and headed out the door. But now that she was here and they were isolated, bound together in this little circle of light, it felt almost otherworldly. Like what was, must be. Like the quiet, dark stars above and a person that you cared about right in front of you.

Jah. She could admit it. She did care about

Samuel, but she didn't know yet where the caring landed in her heart. Samuel had done so much for her already—helped her with the milking, fixed the roof on the house, even helped them track down Charlie when she got out. Now when Mattie looked at him, she didn't see David anymore. And that scared her a bit.

He took a step toward her.

She resisted the urge to step backward. "Next church service, right?" she asked. Her voice trembled a bit on the end. What was wrong with her? Of course she cared for him. He was a member of her family, a fellow human being, a companion and yellow-topper just like herself. That didn't mean it was anything more than that. Especially not until he was right with the church.

"What?" He seemed to be shaken out of his stupor like he had been drawn into the magic surrounding them.

"For you to go before the church. Next service?"

He nodded. But she could tell something was still off. Just a bit.

"Samuel," she started, "if you're not going to…" She couldn't finish.

"I'm going to." He said the words and took another step toward her. This time he was close enough to reach out and grab her elbow.

She should pull away. She should take a step back, two, three. She should turn, tell him good night and walk away. But she stood there in that little bubble of light with him.

"You know, you're beautiful under the stars," he said.

She shook her head. She knew nothing of the sort. It wasn't something she gave much thought or credence to. But somehow when he said it, it seemed as valuable as gold.

"I think you are."

He took another step toward her, close enough now that she had to crane her head back to see him. She really needed to turn and walk away. It was time to leave. Her brain clambered to put her feet into motion, but she stood there still.

"You can tell me to stop."

But she couldn't. She could only bask in the warmth of his eyes, the admiration and the caring she saw there.

He lowered his head and pressed his mouth to hers.

It was past time to turn and walk away. If she had any sense she would be running. She shouldn't be out there, alone in the dark with him. With a man who wasn't her husband. She shouldn't've brought him food. She shouldn't allow him to be so close. And she shouldn't allow him to kiss her. This wasn't how it was done.

But her feet seemed rooted to the spot where she stood in that circle of light they shared.

Finally, she gathered all the strength she could and stepped away from him. The kiss didn't end; it was ended, and she resisted the urge to press the back of her hand against her mouth. No one had ever kissed her other than David. She could no longer say that now. Somehow that thought broke her heart. What was she doing? She let the darkness and the stars, perhaps even the loneliness, get to her.

"Mattie," he started. But he got no further than her name.

"Good night, Samuel." And with that she turned and ran back to the house.

"Are you gonna tell me what happened last night?" Evie asked as she set the butter dish on the table.

"Tell me too," Naomi piped in.

Mattie sent them both a look that clearly said she was saying nothing. But she knew her sisters would hound her until they found out some information. That was sisters.

She had come back to the house after that kiss with Samuel, the tears barely dry on her cheeks. She had wiped them away, told herself to quit being foolish and made her way back into the house.

Sisters always had a way of knowing things a body might not want them to know. Sometimes they found out things that a person might not want them to know that they really needed to know so they could help. This was not one of those things. They couldn't help her. No one could know about the kiss she'd shared with Samuel.

"There's nothing to tell." She grabbed a biscuit and looked at each of them in turn. She put on her best "mom face," that *don't argue with me* expression, that she had seen on her own *mamm* all the years growing up.

Naomi and Evie shared a look, then burst out laughing.

"What's so funny?" Mattie asked.

Gracie and Bethann laughed, enjoying the ruckus even though they had no idea what they were laughing about. The joys of being a child.

"You look just like *Mamm*," Evie said with a small shake of her head and a whimsical smile on her lips.

"I'm glad I can provide you some entertainment this morning." Mattie passed the biscuit she had just buttered to Bethann and started another one for Gracie.

"So are you gonna tell us what happened?" Naomi asked.

"What do you mean what happened? What are you talking about?" She stalled for time.

"Something kept you up all night." Evie shot her a pointed look.

"Who said I was up all night?"

Naomi shook her head. "Please. You've got dark circles under your eyes, and it's apparent you haven't been to sleep at all."

"And my room is right next to yours. I heard you in there all night rummaging around."

"I'm sorry," Mattie said as she passed the biscuit to her youngest and reached for one for herself. "I didn't mean to disturb you."

"So are you going to tell us what happened?" Naomi asked. Mattie shook her head. She couldn't talk about it yet. Not after spending the night fretting over a kiss that in the light of day she doubted even really happened.

Samuel hadn't said a word this morning. He hadn't mentioned it at all. They'd milked the goats in silence, fed and released them, and she'd come back into the house. All without saying even one word to each other. But that in itself told a lot. He was as uncomfortable with the situation as she was. They had tread on holy ground, and there was no coming back from that. Only going forward.

Evie stood and picked up the plate in front of her.

"Where are you going?" Mattie asked.

"I was gonna take this out to Samuel."

"I'll do it." Mattie half stood before Naomi stepped in.

"*I'll* do it," she said. She had her jacket on and was halfway out the door before either one of them could say a word.

A knock sounded on the barn door, the sound so unfamiliar that Samuel almost didn't recognize it for what it was. Who knocked on a barn door? He turned from where he was cleaning the mare's hooves to find Naomi Ebersol standing there. She held a plate of steaming breakfast in one hand.

Samuel released the mare and patted her on the back for coming out of the stall. He stopped a good twenty paces from Naomi.

"Breakfast," she said without any greeting. She indicated the plate she held.

"*Danki,*" he said. "But I believe the proper procedure is to set it down. Any old hay bale will work." He pulled out a rag and wiped his hands.

She did as he asked, then turned back to him, arms crossed, lips pressed together. He recognized the pose for exactly what it was: protection.

He finished wiping his hands and stuffed the

rag back into the waistband of his pants. "I'm not here to hurt her."

"*Jah?* Then why are you here?"

"I told her. She didn't tell you?" If she hadn't told her sisters the explanation he had given, what hope did he have of ever convincing her to go through with it?

"She told us. Now, I want to know the real reason you're here." Her eyes flashed, aqua-colored fire, ice-cold and scorching hot. Heaven help anyone who stood in Naomi Ebersol's way.

"I'm here because I promised David."

"What if I don't believe that?" She widened her stance just a bit, as if digging in for the long game.

"I can't help that," he told her calmly. He knew going in he would get pushback, resistance from her family, from her, from the community. But he was going to make good on that promise. She would need someone to care for her and the girls. What else was there to think about?

"What happened between the two of you last night?"

The question caught him off guard. Resistance was one thing, protection another, but that kiss...

It wasn't something he wanted to share with anyone. He was still reeling that it had happened at all. He'd been living out among the *Englisch* too long, he supposed, and they didn't abide by the same rules.

He swallowed hard. "Nothing," he lied, and he felt the twitch of that spot under his left eye that Mattie had told him about. Thankfully, Naomi didn't know his tell. Because to call that kiss nothing...

It was something all right. But it wasn't something he had figured out yet. He had come back home with the intention of marrying Mattie. Everyone knew what a marriage meant. But he hadn't thought about that part of the relationship. Hadn't thought about anything but making sure his brother's family was cared for now and always. Maybe something like *that*, like bedroom...appeal, could come with time. This wasn't about love or desire; it was about fulfilling a promise, and to have that attraction thrown in... Well, it took his breath away.

He managed to drag his gaze back to Naomi's. She lifted her chin a notch. "*Jah*, that's what she said too. Funny how I don't believe either one of you."

Samuel gave a shrug that he intended to be negligent but somehow felt awkward and stiff, as if his joints needed to be oiled before they could perform the action. "I can't stop you from what you're going to think."

"You're right about that one. But if you hurt her…" She shook her head as if she didn't want to be in his shoes. "I may be Amish, but you will regret it. When it comes to my sister…" She left her words dangling in the air between them, then she spun on her heel and left the barn before he could think of anything to say in return.

Yet he understood. He would feel the same if anyone tried to hurt his sister.

Chapter Eleven

"You suppose he's going to his sister's today?" Evie asked, looking toward the living room window as if she could see Samuel from there.

It was Thursday, Thanksgiving, and they were just sitting down to eat. It wasn't a traditional Thanksgiving meal with turkey and dressing and all the other trimmings that people liked to have together on this day.

Evie had put a beef roast in the oven early that morning. It had been slowly baking since then, its wonderful aroma filling the house and making Mattie hungry all day long.

"I don't figure Joshua Glick would allow that. Plus, they're probably either going to her *mamm*'s house or the Glick family's." Or who knew? They might be at the same wedding her family was at. "Bethann, if you keep eating the rolls, you're not gonna want any supper." She took the warm yeast roll from her daughter's hand and set it on her plate. "Wait for the rest of us. You know the rules."

"So he's probably out in the barn," Evie continued. She was using one crutch today to help her get along while still setting the table.

Mattie marveled at her sister and how she just kept going despite the roadblocks and challenges she faced every day. Evie was part of the reason why Mattie could get up in the morning. Evie's courage and her daughters' sweet faces. Those were what kept her going.

And just like that, Samuel's face popped into her head. She pushed the image away. She didn't want to think about him. She surely didn't want to think about him in the barn alone on Thanksgiving Day. True, it wasn't an important holiday for the Amish. Partially because so many people scheduled weddings during the month of November and Amish weddings were traditionally on Tuesdays and Thursdays and partially, she supposed, because they gave thanks every day. It was very important to them as a community to continually give thanks for the Lord's blessings. Setting a day aside for it just seemed like…overkill.

And speaking of overkill…

"What are you saying, Evie?" Mattie pinned

her sister with a quick look. She knew what she wanted, but Mattie wanted to hear her say it.

"I don't think we should just take him a plate today." She bit her lip and looked to the two youngest ones seated there. Gracie wouldn't remember it, and chances were Bethann wouldn't either in a year or two. But come next Sunday at church she might, and then what would happen?

Nothing. Who was going to listen to a three-year-old?

"If that's what you want to do." Mattie couldn't take responsibility for this decision. Probably and mostly because she wanted him to come in so badly. She'd seen him that morning at the milking. They had done their thing, working side by side to get the animals ready, milking them, getting them put back out into the pasture—which resulted in them running right back into their heated barn—and storing the milk in the propane-run coolers. She had been finding this week that the more time she spent with Samuel, the more time she wanted to spend with Samuel. And quite frankly, she was beginning to find the truth of it frightening. The last thing, the very last thing, she wanted to do was to depend on someone again like she had depended on David.

Her whole life she'd been taught to grow up, get married, be a partner to her husband, but she found out that marriage was so much more than that. Aspects that she never thought she would have again: companionship, combined faith, just the knowledge that someone was there for her at the end of the day.

"I just feel like it's the right thing to do," Evie said. She stopped, seemed to think about it a moment. "I hope it's okay for me to say this, but I feel like it's what David would've wanted."

She was exactly right. Mattie shook her head, but couldn't keep the smile from twitching at the corners of her mouth. "Go get him."

"Are you sure about this?" Samuel asked, easing in the door just a few minutes later.

"I'm sure," Mattie said. She hadn't been sure of anything in months. Not since David died. And especially not since Samuel Byler had shown up on her farm. But of this, she was certain.

"You can wash up in the bathroom down the hall." Evie pointed the way.

Samuel hung his coat on the peg by the door and made his way down to clean up.

No. Not *his* coat. David's coat.

It was Samuel's coat now, and suddenly it hit her, the problem with it all. She was afraid that by inviting Samuel in, David would somehow get gobbled up in the process. There would be nothing that belonged to him any longer. Not the house or the farm where his children lived, even his coat or his hat, which was still on the shelf in the closet.

She set the bowl of corn on the table with a loud thunk.

"Are you okay?" Evie asked. "What's wrong?"

Mattie shook her head, even as tears rose in her eyes. She had to get ahold of herself. Pregnancy hormones, grief, shunnings—it was a lot to have to deal with at one time.

"Not the baby?" Evie's voice was filled with concern.

Mattie quickly pulled herself together. She blinked back the tears and smiled at her sister. "Not the baby. Everything's fine. I just had a, I don't know, moment of sadness."

Evie nodded sagely. "I suppose that's normal."

"I suppose," Mattie murmured in return. She was saved from saying anything else as Samuel returned from the bathroom, the hair around his face slightly damp where he had washed his face. Then she realized that he probably hadn't had a shower in a while, at least not since he'd been in town. Most likely he had taken some sort of sponge bath at his campsite. That couldn't feel good. Not clean like a person should be, yet she couldn't invite him in for that. Dinner was enough.

You could if you said you were going to marry him. He would be her fiancé then.

She pushed the thought away; it was too soon for all that. Way too soon.

She moved to take her place at the head of the table.

Gracie squealed when she saw him. And Bethann shot Mattie a cheeky smile. *"Jah,"* the little girl said. "Samuel not *Dat* here."

"That's right," Mattie said. But she didn't say anything else. Sometimes explanations were just too much, and children took things at face value if you didn't overexplain them. At least, that was what she was hoping for this time.

"I glad," Bethann said with a firm nod of her head, the kind of nod that almost dared anyone to say differently.

Everyone at the table laughed, including Gracie who had no idea what she was laughing about. Then Samuel raised his glass toward all of them. "I'm glad I'm here too."

It was perhaps the most pathetic excuse she had ever concocted in order to talk to someone. But Samuel was still out in the barn and would be for another few minutes, checking the temperature on the vats and making sure that everything was right with the milk before leaving the barn for the day.

She had checked her cheeses, checked the coolers in the store and helped Evie set out a spread of cold cuts and cheese to eat before bed. Now here she stood, headed for the door, carrying a little plastic container with a piece of sweet potato pie nestled inside.

But after today, eating that meal with him at the table, watching him interact with her girls, noticing more and more the differences between him and his brother made her feel more connected to him than she ever had. It was beginning to scare her. Not in a bad way, but as sort of a caution. And only because he still had matters to clear up before any further relationship could happen between the two of them. Actually, they had taken things a little far already, time to take a step back, start getting everything in line. Then who knew where it could lead?

"You know you don't have to take a piece of pie out there and pretend that you need to give him dessert." Evie shot her a pointed look. "You can just go out there."

Mattie gave a sheepish grin. "I suppose not. But since I'm going, why not bring pie?"

Evie laughed and shook her head. "Go on with you, then."

Mattie grabbed her coat from the hook beside the door. She tied her scarf around her head and stepped out into the chilly November evening.

Temperatures had been steadily dropping, and more than anything she hated the thought of Samuel sleeping in a tent. The thing probably had holes in it. He told her that he had bought it in a secondhand shop. How good could it be? It didn't look very sturdy when she had seen it the last time she'd been out to his campsite, but she hadn't been looking for such things then. She was too busy trying to determine if he was for real. But after today she knew he was. All the way straight to her bones. She knew it.

The confidence she felt when leaving the house slowly seeped out of her the closer she got to the barn. Her footsteps began to slow. She had pie. She could lead with that. Then what? It wasn't like she could come right out and ask him if he meant what he said about marrying her. She had asked him before and he had answered. But now, it seemed too forward.

She took a deep breath, pausing at the doorway, trying to come up with something to say, wondering what to say, thinking of nothing new to tell him other than she wanted to see him one last time before he went back to his campsite.

And she had pie.

Almost hesitantly, she pushed open the barn door and slipped inside. "Samuel?" she called.

He stepped out from the second stall, his head

swiveling in her direction. "Mattie? Is something wrong?"

She held up the container holding the sweet potato pie. "There's one piece of pie left. I thought you might enjoy having it."

"Danki," he returned with a small nod. "That didn't answer my question though. Is there something wrong?"

She shook her head. "Just thinking about things. I'm sorry that I can't invite you to stay in the house. I just wish things were…different."

He had a faraway look on his face that Mattie didn't quite know how to interpret. He got that same look every time they talked about God and him coming back to the church. *"Jah,"* he said. "Me too. But soon." His words held a note of promise but nothing more. That made her just a tad wary.

She pushed those feelings away. She was just being paranoid now. The Bible told them plainly not to borrow trouble from tomorrow. Today had enough problems all on its own.

And today was Thanksgiving. It was a day to be thankful and enjoy family, and that was just what she had done.

She set the dish containing the pie on the nearest hay bale and gave another small nod in his direction. "Okay then." She started inching back toward the door. "I guess I'll just…"

"If you're sure everything's all right," he pressed once more.

She nodded. "What are you doing in there?" She inclined her head toward the door of the stall. *Jah*, she was changing the subject. But she had something she wanted to ask and she just couldn't seem to get the words running around inside her head to actually slow down where she could ask them.

He turned back, gave a small glance toward that last stall. "Making a bed for Goldie."

"Danki," she said. David's dog had been a constant companion since his death, but she was getting up in years. Arthritis had taken hold of her joints and she seemed to move a bit slower every day.

Samuel's mouth twisted into a sorrowful smile that looked sadder than just about anything she had ever seen. "I don't think she's going to be with us much longer."

"I'm surprised she's lasted this long," Mattie said. "I thought we were going to lose her this summer and then after David died, she seemed to hang on just to protect me."

"I made her a bed in here so she could stay warm and have fresh hay away from the other animals. I know she goes in with the goats, but I think they tend to bully her a bit."

Mattie gave a small chuckle through her own

sadness. "*Jah*, they can be that way. And she's too much of a sweetheart to fight back. This cold weather really bothers her."

"Now she has a place where she can be out of the wind and away from them."

His thoughtfulness had tears pricking at the back of her eyes.

"Just when you come out in the mornings—" He faltered. "It's just that…" He stopped once more. "I mean—"

She held up one hand to stop his words. "I know what you're saying. If I come out in the morning, I'm prepared." But not really.

The dog had been a part of her life so long now she barely could remember it without her. Goldie had been four or five when Samuel left. Then she had moved with David when he built this house for the two of them to live in after they got married. Two had become four, then three again. Add in a goat. Very soon they would have to subtract a dog. Life math was hard.

"If something does happen," Samuel started once more, "I'll take care of it for you. Everything."

She swallowed the lump of sadness in her throat and nodded. "*Danki*, Samuel," she said. "I really appreciate that."

He gave a nod.

She paused one heartbeat longer. She wanted to ask him if he truly was going to step in front of the congregation, confess his sins and do all the things he needed to do to get himself right with the church. But somehow it didn't seem to be the right time. She wanted to ask, because she knew in her heart of hearts, she was falling for him. Sure, some of it could just be the sheer loneliness that she felt each night, going to bed in a house made for two, but there was just one there. She missed sharing the days, events and funny things the girls did, the outlandish things her sisters said and all the other tiny aspects of her day. At first it had been David she missed. Now she just missed someone being there.

"Are you sure you're okay?" he asked.

She gave a reassuring nod. "I'm fine. I'll see you tomorrow, Samuel. Enjoy the pie." On that note, she let herself out of the barn, and hustled back to the house. Not once did she turn around.

She was a coward. That much was certain. But she couldn't continue to ask him and ask him if he was going to show up at the next church meeting. So instead they talked about everything else: the girls, Goldie, goats and a little about his family. The afternoon just before the church service that week, on Saturday, he pulled her to one side.

"I know it's cold out," he started. "But can you talk to me for a little bit?"

Something urgent in his eyes sent her heart plummeting to her feet. But she quickly recovered. It was just that old anxiety coming back, too many loves lost, miles broken, to think the tone of his voice could mean anything but. Yet she knew it didn't have to be one of those. It could merely be a hard conversation.

She managed to swallow back her fears. "Of course." She gestured toward the goat barn. "Where it's warm?"

His mouth twitched into a smile of relief, though *smile* was a very generous word. "That sounds great."

She walked in front of him toward the heated goat barn. She could tell he was reluctant and that sense of dread returned once more. She turned right as they got to the door. "Samuel." She held her hands up in front of her, almost touching him, but not quite.

He reached for her, but stopped short of clasping her fingers.

"You don't have to tell me things that—" She didn't know how to finish what she was saying. She wanted him to tell her everything. She wanted to know about the years he had been gone. She felt he had a burden on his heart and that the only way to lighten it would be to share it. Of course, the best way would be to share it with God, but she understood how a hard life could bruise one's faith. She wouldn't believe he had lost his. He wouldn't have returned if he had. But coming back, like leaving, was not to be taken lightly.

He reached around her and opened the door.

Mattie waited only a second more before slipping inside.

She was proud of the goat barn that David had built. *Jah*, to some it might seem a little strange that it was almost like an indoor pasture/playground where the goats could climb, eat hay, jump on things and even teeter totter on an imbalanced slide. Every time David came home with the new idea for the room, she laughed until she walked in and saw the goats enjoying it immensely.

But the best thing they had done was heating it. For now she could stand here with Samuel amid all the bleats and cries and the goats that rushed around them, wondering if milking time had come early. But she could stand here with him out of range from the prying ears of her sisters and hopefully he could unburden his heart.

"I'm not coming to church tomorrow." His words were so quietly spoken she wondered for a moment if she had imagined them. She swung her attention back to his face.

"You're not?" Mattie asked. He had really said those words, but a part of her prayed that he would give her a confused look and ask her what she was talking about. That prayer wasn't answered.

"I can't." He closed his eyes and sucked in a breath. His shoulders trembled. She waited for him to continue; she didn't want to press, not when a part of her so strongly wanted to reach up and touch the smooth line of his cheekbones.

He opened those blue eyes once more, and she could see the remorse, the sadness and the regret lurking there, emotions he didn't want to reveal but that seemed to fill him up so much he couldn't hide them. "I have something I need to tell you. First. And then maybe after that. I—I fully meant to go before now but—"

She laid her hand on his chest just over where his heart pounded. He was as anxious as she was. "Whatever it is, Samuel, just tell me."

He reached up and clasped her hand in his own, removing her fingers from his chest even as he held on. "You know how I was, growing up. I mean, you don't know how it was for me, but you know how everyone felt."

She nodded. It was no big secret that Samuel had been restless. He had been for as long as she had known the word. He had left three times between sixteen and nineteen. Then when he turned twenty, he and David joined the church together. That vow had lasted two years, then he left again, only to come back a few short weeks ago.

"It's hard out there for Amish," he admitted. "Everyone knows we're sheltered, that our lives are constructed to continue the status quo of the community. But you can't survive like that among the *Englisch*. When you don't have schooling and all the other things that they have." He shook his head. "What I'm trying to say is I didn't have a lot of job skills, and I didn't want to just be a waiter or fry cook. The only true skill I had was construction."

Mattie nodded, encouraging him to continue.

"I ended up in business with this man. I guess the biggest problem was I thought I knew what I was doing. I thought I could trust people. I thought I could read people, but life in an Amish community doesn't always prepare you for some of the characters you meet out there."

"What happened?" Her question was barely whispered. In fact, she spoke so softly she wasn't even sure he could hear her over the noise all the goats were making. Evidently, he had for he continued.

"To make a long story short he was not a level businessman and when push came to shove, he set me up to take the fall for his various illegal business practices."

"Take the fall?"

"It means take the blame."

"I see." Taking the blame didn't sound like any type of light affair.

"I spent four years in prison for his crimes."

"Oh, Samuel." She didn't know what to say. Most likely there weren't any words to make the situation better.

He gave a negligent shrug. "It happens."

She shook her head. "But that it happened to you."

"There's more," he said.

"Okay." She waited for him to continue.

"I guess this is the hardest part of all. See, I pled guilty to get a lighter sentence. A plea deal they call it. So I didn't have to serve as long, and I didn't have to go to trial. It was easier that way, but harder at the same time."

"I see," she said even though she didn't really. It was one thing to not fight back if someone tried to get them to break their vow of passivity and another to just not fight back at all. It seemed like that was what he did.

"I know you don't understand why I did it. You're not the only one, but it doesn't matter now. It's over and done. I did what I did. I served my time and I'm a free man now."

"Why didn't you tell me this before?" It didn't make a difference to her that he had been in prison. She had seen the magazines in the grocery store and heard talk about people who had gone to prison for crimes they hadn't committed. Some of these people had been set free years later after new evidence arose. Even just the few stories she had heard made her realize that anyone could potentially go to prison for any crime, whether they committed it or not. She no more believed Samuel guilty than she did herself. But the fact that he hadn't told her before now hurt her somehow. She couldn't quite explain it; it just did.

"Why didn't you tell me this before?" she asked again.

He had come in claiming that he was going to marry her. He would get himself back right with the church and yet he harbored this secret. The secret itself didn't hold much against him for her, but that he held it and didn't tell her, that was the part she truly couldn't understand.

"I guess I've been away too long," he said. "A lot of people out there will hold something like this against you whether you're guilty or not. Most don't even ask the difference."

"Do you think so little of me?"

He was shaking his head before she even finished. "No, no, no, Mattie, no. It's not you. It's me. I just have a lot of adjustments to make. I'm not used to people forgiving so easily."

"You grew up with it your entire life."

He closed his eyes for just a moment, then opened them once again.

And once again she could see that remorse there. She knew he had suffered, and she could see the building regrets. "I did. You're absolutely right. But standing here today, that all seems like a dream, far away and untouchable."

They stood there for a moment, the goats milling about, trying to urge them to play though neither one of them was in a playful mood.

"Your mother," Mattie said. "Does she know this?"

"I know there are a couple of rumors floating around about me, but none of the ones I've heard are correct. So I don't suppose she does. I went to prison long after *Dat* declared me dead."

"And how did you know to come here?"

He sent her a rueful smile. "Right before I was released, I saw the newspaper clipping about David's death and your goat farm. And I remembered my promise."

"I can't believe he would make you promise something like that and not ever once mention it to me." She couldn't keep the thread of hurt from her tone.

"He didn't expect to die."

"I suppose not."

She turned to walk out of the barn, leaving him no choice but to follow her or stay. Right now she needed time to assimilate all this information, put it in an order that she could understand. Each part of it was reasonable enough, but she needed the whole picture.

"Mattie," he called when she was halfway to the porch steps. She stopped, turned around slowly.

"I promised my brother," he began, "but I would marry you today without that promise."

Chapter Twelve

"Are you going to tell me? Or are you going to keep me guessing?" Evie peered at Mattie across the top of her crocheting.

Mattie needed to be working on her project as well. She was knitting a scarf for Samuel. She should be working on it instead of staring off into space, rubbing Charlie's velvety soft ear between her thumb and forefinger as she contemplated all that she had learned about Samuel.

"Okay." She sighed. "I guess you'll find out sooner or later but… Evie, you can't tell anyone, okay? Not even Naomi."

The front door opened and Naomi walked in, hearing the last bit, including her name. "Tell Naomi what?"

Wasn't that always the way it was?

The Ebersol sisters ran in clusters of three—Mattie, Evie and Naomi, then Priscilla, Lizzie and Sarah Ann. That was most likely due to the fact that was how their rooms were split up. Their mother separated them oldest to youngest down the middle. Since Priscilla was the younger twin, she became the oldest of the second group of Ebersol girls. Until she married, that was. Now she lived in the *dawdihaus* attached to their father's house, having sold her property when her husband died. It kept her close so the family could help her with the babies. So far it was working out for everyone.

"Mattie was just about to reveal all of Samuel's secrets."

"Evie," Mattie chastised. "I'm not telling all his secrets. It's just that he did tell me something, and it's gonna come out in church. Not this week, but definitely in a couple of weeks when he goes up in front of everyone. And if I tell you, you just can't tell anyone else. I don't know how many people he wants knowing right now."

"What difference does it make since everybody's gonna know in a couple of weeks anyway?" Naomi asked.

Mattie turned to Evie. "And this is why I didn't want you to tell Naomi."

Naomi hung her bonnet and coat up by the door and threw her hands in the air. "Fine. Don't tell me. See if I care. Where are the girls?"

"In the playroom, and they're finally playing nice for once. Don't go disturb them."

"I see. You don't want to tell me your secret, and I can't play with the children."

"What is wrong with you?" Evie asked.

"What's got you in such a bad mood?"

Naomi closed her eyes for a moment, sucked in a deep breath as if trying to soothe her own inner self. "Nothing." She opened her eyes once more. "I'm fine. Really." She gave them a forced smile.

Mattie knew this was the part when she should stop and question Naomi further about the situation, whatever it was. But honestly, right now she just wasn't up to it. She had enough troubles without adding her sister's to her own. She hated herself for that selfishness.

Naomi came around and sat in the chair opposite Mattie. "I promise I won't tell anyone."

"Your prayer *kapp* is crooked," Evie said.

"For pity's sake," Naomi cried and tried to straighten it without getting up and looking in the mirror.

"I know why or at least one of the reasons why Samuel hasn't been back to Millers Creek in years. Four of them at least."

"Jah?" Evie said.

Naomi dropped her hands in her lap and gave her full attention to Mattie.

"He's been in prison for something he didn't do."

Her sisters stared at her incredulously.

"I knew it had to be something like that." Evie shook her head.

"That poor man," Naomi said. "This is what they warned us about, isn't it? Getting out in the *Englisch* world and being taken advantage of. That's what happened to him, right?"

Mattie nodded. "He went into business with a man who framed him for shoddy workmanship and embezzlement. So he pled guilty to the charges for a lighter sentence. That way he wouldn't have to go to trial."

"How long ago was this?" Naomi asked.

"He said he just got out."

Evie slowly shook her head. "It's a shame really, but now he's back and that's a good thing, *jah*?"

"He's having trouble gathering his thoughts and feelings so he can go before the church. He's not going to be at church on Sunday."

"The bishop is not going to let him wait much longer." Naomi shot Mattie a knowing look.

Mattie scratched Charlie's head, right between her eyes. The goat stretched out, laid her head on Mattie's lap and started lightly snoring. Oh, to be able to sleep like that.

"No, if he doesn't start soon, then he'll have to go." And the mere thought of him leaving made her stomach hurt, made her throat hurt, made her heart hurt. In such a short period of time, she had come to depend on him. Not just for work, but for companionship in the work, someone to talk to. She could talk to her sisters, but they cared as little about goats as they did about any other farm animal. But Samuel seemed to listen. He seemed to care about the creatures, how to make cheese and all the other things that she had going on. It was as if he knew: since it was important to David, it should be important to him. Or maybe because it was important to Mattie, it had become important to Samuel. But all that would go away if he didn't get himself back right with the church. And soon.

"Hello? Sister? Mattie? Are you there?"

Mattie pulled her thoughts away from worrying over Samuel and the church and instead trained her gaze on Naomi. "What?"

"So good to see you back from vacation."

Mattie shook her head. "What do you want, Naomi?"

"How long have you been sitting here?" Naomi asked.

"I don't know. I set the girls up at the table with a puzzle and I came here and sat down."

And started thinking, but she didn't say those words out loud.

"Look." Naomi gestured to Mattie's lap.

Mattie jumped to her feet, knocking Charlie to one side. The goat bleated her disapproval and scampered off under the coffee table. "You better run, you beast," Mattie said. She smoothed a hand over the gaping, still damp hole in her dress.

"Did you know she was there?" Naomi asked.

Mattie sighed and shook her head. "She started off licking my hand and then licking my belly. Like she was, I don't know, acknowledging the baby. I guess I'm being silly. But then I guess she started nibbling, and I started thinking. And I lost track of what she was doing." And she had eaten straight through her apron and dress. Ruining both.

"You just had to have a pygmy goat," Naomi teased.

"I know," Mattie said. "She's a bad girl. But I do love her so." Just maybe a little less when she ate through her clothes. Or ran out of the house and hid on top of the buggy so no one could find her. Or ate the bishop's wife's cherry pie while she was trying to eat it herself. Little things like that.

"Mattie!" Evie came stomping down the stairs, one hand on the rail and the other braced against her crutch. In the crook of that arm she held a familiar piece of black material.

"What's wrong?" Why did everything always seem to happen at once?

"I was getting our clothes ready for church tomorrow and look." With that she held up the dress that Mattie now realized was her church dress and half the sleeve was gone. Eaten. No doubt by a mischievous goat.

"Charlie!" Mattie groaned.

The goat bleated in return.

Mattie turned to Naomi. "Do we have any more of that material left?" If they did, they would only have to remake the sleeve and sew it on. Perfect.

Naomi shook her head sadly and grimaced. "No, don't you remember? We used every scrap we had of it."

Not perfect.

Repairing the dress was out of the question.

That was two dresses in one day. A record even for Charlie.

"What happened to the dress you've got on?" Evie called.

"The same thing that happened to that one."

"I can see about letting out one of the others," Evie offered.

Mattie knew it would do no good. This baby seemed to be growing at an alarming rate compared to her two girls. It made her wonder if this was a boy, but she stopped those thoughts before they could really get going. All the doctors said babies were usually bigger in subsequent pregnancies and neither one of her girls was tiny. Both were over eight pounds. Letting her other black dresses out, that wasn't going to happen with this baby.

Evie looked to the clock on the mantel. She bit her lip and turned back to Mattie. "I can run into town and get the material and make one really quick. I mean if that's all I do, and you guys take care of supper and the girls, then I should have it done by the morning."

"I hate to ask you to do that," Mattie said.

Evie laughed. "You didn't ask me. I offered."

"It's a lot of work," she countered.

Evie smiled. "It's a good thing I like to sew then."

Samuel wiped his palms down the front of his pants, then knocked on Mattie's door. The day was cloudy, overcast and cold, and yet he felt the sheen of perspiration on his forehead.

It was understandable after everything he had been through, but it was over. It was time to move forward.

He had taken the afternoon off and walked to the bishop's house. Samuel had wanted to talk with him about his plan to get back right with the church. About when he would kneel before the congregation, what he could do, and how he was to repent. They had laid it all out, then Samuel had asked for the impossible: one more church cycle to get his mind right and ready.

But even then, he knew it wouldn't be enough time. There was too much space between him and God these days. He had done everything in his power to get back to where he needed to be. Where he had been his whole life. Until...

It wasn't that he didn't believe. Only a fool could look at the blue sky, the beautiful green grass, frolicking goats and babies' smiles and not know that there was a power above them all. It was the will of that power that had him with his back turned. It was something he had been taught his entire life. God's will. God's will. God's will.

He hadn't questioned it when his grandmother died. He hadn't questioned it when a friend drowned in the creek. He hadn't questioned it when his cousin fell out of the barn loft and broke his back, paralyzing him for the rest of his life. He had taken it all in stride. God's will, but then Emma—

The thought remained incomplete as the door before him opened.

"Samuel." Mattie glanced behind her, then

deftly stuck one foot in the crack of the door and prevented her goat from escaping. It was quite impressive.

She nudged the goat back with her foot, then eased out, as easily as a woman who was seven months pregnant could ease out of anywhere. She shut the door behind her.

Samuel pulled his hat from his head and stepped backward. He gestured to the yard behind him. "I should—"

Mattie shook her head. "No. This is fine."

He should have known. His own mother might not let him on the porch at the house he grew up in, but Mattie had her own set of beliefs.

"I just got back from the bishop's house," he started. His voice cracked on the last word. "I just wanted to let you know. I'm going to be at the next church service. We've agreed on everything and after that..." He couldn't finish. After that he would serve his shunning and then he would marry Mattie. The amazing thing was that what had started off to be the fulfillment of a brother's promise had become so much more. He never thought that he would love again. How could he? When a person had been afforded such a special love, they couldn't expect that to happen twice in a lifetime. And yet every time he was close to Mattie, he felt that same connection.

"If this is about the other night…" she started. Pink rose into her cheeks, color that he knew had nothing to do with the cold.

The kiss. Actually, it had a lot to do with the other night and that kiss they shared. But not in the way she meant. He intended to marry her and not because he promised his brother. Not any longer anyway. He wanted to marry her because he had fallen in love with her

There. He admitted it. Somehow, someway, by some act of the Divine, he had fallen in love with Mattie Byler. He had fallen in love with her and her daughters and her silly goat and her farm and her sisters and everything else about her. The problem was that the only way to Mattie was through God. He wasn't sure his heart was in that one.

"No," he said as emphatically as possible. "That was forward," he said.

She shook her head. "You don't have to explain."

"But I do," he said. "I know all the things I said when I came here. And they're all true. David did make me promise and I am here to fulfill that promise, but since I got here…" He shook his head. "Since I got here, things weren't at all like I thought. I have begun to care about you, Mattie. A lot. And I just want you to know that you mean a great deal to me, not even as my brother's wife, but as a beautiful person. One I want to spend more time with."

He said the words and realized he should've said more. He should have said that he wanted to spend the rest of his life with her, that he wanted to spend the rest of their lives together. That once a person finds love they have to grab ahold with both hands and not let go because who knew how long they would have it?

But he wasn't sure if she was ready to hear that yet. He wasn't sure if he was ready to say that yet. He kept telling himself they had time. They had time, but that alone went against grabbing ahold of love with both hands and not letting go. It couldn't be both ways. And once again, he was back to God. To letting go of past hurts and perceived betrayals at the hand of a higher power.

He waited for her to say something, anything. But she just stood there and watched him, one hand pressed to her round belly. He had never seen her do that before, acknowledge the baby in front of him. In fact, he didn't ever remember seeing a pregnant Amish woman do that. He knew the ins and outs and the whys they didn't openly acknowledge their babies in public, actions so different from *Englisch* women, so he immediately grew concerned.

"Is everything okay?" He nodded to where her hand rested.

She swallowed hard, briefly closed her eyes before opening them again. "*Jah.* Just—" She broke off.

"She's moving around?" He said the words before he remembered who he was talking to, thought about how forward they were.

Mattie nodded.

"Can I—" He took a step toward her before he thought twice about it, before he registered the surprised look on her face.

She held her ground and gave a small nod.

He pressed his hand to the spot on her belly where hers had been. It had been awhile, but he knew the wonder for what it was. The marvel of life and birth and God.

He could feel the tiny infant moving around, could feel their eager kicks and tumbles. And he wanted to stay that way for as long as he possibly could, his hand on her belly, witnessing this astounding new life.

But he had overstepped with this. He had overstepped with his kiss; perhaps there would be another time in the future.

He reluctantly removed his hand from her belly and took a step back.

"You think it's a girl?"

It was perhaps the last question he thought

she would ask. He never dreamed that she would continue to acknowledge the baby in front of him. A part of him hoped that was a connection between them that was growing.

He gave a small shrug. "I don't know. It just came out like that."

She nodded. "Thanks for telling me about the bishop."

"You're welcome." He stood there smiling like a fool.

She gestured to the door behind her. "I've got stuff on the stove," she said and gave an awkward laugh.

He returned it with a nervous chuckle of his own. "I'll just go—" He jerked a thumb over his shoulder toward the barn. Everything was caught up, even with the afternoon he'd spent at the bishop's house. But he couldn't continue to stand on her front porch and talk about nothing. And they couldn't talk about anything more serious until he went before the church.

"I'll see you at the next milking," she said. Then slipped inside before he could say another word.

Mattie shut the door behind her and leaned her back against it. Eyes closed, she let out a long sigh.

"What's the matter?"

Mattie startled as Evie's voice sounded from the doorway leading to the kitchen.

"Why are you so jumpy?"

Mattie shook her head. She couldn't tell her sister. Not yet. But it seemed as if Samuel had just declared his love for her. What else could he have meant?

Jah, it was forward, but she could only chalk that up to the time he spent in the *Englisch* world. He hadn't quite adjusted back to Amish ways, especially in such matters. She wondered if he ever would.

Not that it mattered. He had said he was beginning to care for her. That in itself made her heart sing. She never thought she would ever say such a thing again. Not about loving again, not after David. Not at all. Much less after such a short period of time. But somehow it seemed that her time with David was in its own little box. It was a completed cycle of when they started to date until they got married and had children and then his accident. And somehow in her heart that was how it felt. It wasn't that she lamented time with David because she knew, in God's ultimate plan, her time with David was finished.

But did that mean it was time for her and Samuel? She had no idea.

She was jumping ahead of herself. He had

to confess before the church, and that wasn't going to happen for a couple of weeks yet. Just before Christmas.

"Are you gonna tell me who was at the door or are you gonna just make me guess?" Evie looked up from her sewing machine with knowing eyes.

Mattie pushed herself back right. "It was Samuel. Just as you know it was."

Who else would have been knocking at their door? Who else would have been knocking at the door that she wasn't allowed to let inside the house?

"And what did Samuel want?" Evie pressed.

Just about that time, Naomi came down the stairs with the girls.

"Samuel was here?"

Evie turned to their sister. "She didn't let him in."

Naomi nodded and Mattie couldn't determine if it was a nod of approval or disappointment. "Is he coming to church tomorrow?"

It was the question on everybody's lips. When was Samuel going to bend his knee and get himself back right with the church?

If he truly wanted to marry her as he said he did, wouldn't it be sooner rather than later?

Mattie pushed that thought aside. He had explained it to her. He had big issues to work through. The bishop wouldn't take it easy on him. Leroy Peachey considered leaving the community a grave misstep. More than one soul had thought they could do better outside, only to come back and fall to their knees.

"No," she said simply. She fully intended to leave it at that. She made her way into the kitchen.

"Where are you going?" Naomi asked, following behind her. The girls toddled behind her.

"I need to get the soup on so it can be ready by supper time," she explained simply. Then she scooped Gracie into her arms, administering several neck kisses, which in turn blessed her with a rash of giggles. Then she kissed Bethann on the top of the head and placed Gracie back on her tiny feet.

She should be ashamed using the girls like that to create a diversion, but she wasn't ready to talk to her sisters about this. Highly unusual. Normally, she wanted to talk to her sisters first off about something, anything, everything. But this…

Samuel had his own secrets, that much she knew, but she supposed that a man who had been to prison would naturally have a few. Things that he didn't want to tell anyone about life on the inside. She could understand that. And she would honor that. She wouldn't press him for answers; she wouldn't ask questions too hard for him to answer. She would let him make his way. It was the only thing she could do. Except now that she felt like she was falling in love with him, the quicker he got through all this, the quicker they could get married.

Not that she was in a big hurry to remarry. She wouldn't want to cause too many raised eyebrows in the community. After all, she would be marrying her husband's twin brother. She was sure that would send a few tongues wagging. But the thought of making her family whole again was almost too irresistible to turn away from.

Mattie reached under the counter and pulled out her big iron pot.

"What are you not telling us?" Naomi asked.

She set the pot on her stovetop but didn't turn to face her sister.

"I told you everything," she said simply. "What's there not to tell? He has to work through a few things. I'm sure this time of year is hard, being Christmas and everything. Plus, who wants to do that on Christmas Day?"

The wonderful thing about this year was that Christmas was on Sunday, a church Sunday for their district. It didn't happen often and so it was a special treat to be able to go to church and worship on the Lord's birthday.

"And that's it?"

"Of course." Mattie moved to the refrigerator. She pulled out the chicken for tonight's supper along with two cheese sticks.

"Why do I get the feeling it's not that at all?" Naomi pressed.

Mattie shrugged. She set the chicken on the counter and handed the cheese sticks to her sister. "Will you take the girls and sit them down at the table? Here's a snack to hold them over until supper's ready."

Naomi looked at the cheese sticks and back at her.

Mattie waited for her sister to kick up a fuss, start to question everything she was asking her to do, asking questions that maybe Mattie didn't have the answer for.

But Naomi took the cheese sticks and the girls without question and moved into the dining area.

Mattie turned back toward the stove and drew in a deep breath. She had told Samuel that she understood his hesitations, but in truth she didn't. Not quite. He had come stating that he was going to marry her and set her family back to rights. Yet he hadn't taken the first necessary steps in order to make that a reality.

"I thought you were making soup," Evie said.

Mattie whirled around, caught thinking about

things she had no answer to, mulling over problems that seemed to have no solution. At least not at this time they didn't.

Stuck. That was what she was.

"I thought you were sewing." The words came out harsher than she had intended. But she felt cornered. Her sister standing there in the doorway watching her with wary eyes. It wasn't her fault though.

"Are you gonna tell us what's going on or not?" Naomi took a step forward.

Mattie wanted to go backward, but the stove was behind her. There was nowhere to go.

She had nowhere to go and only one option. And that was to tell the truth. Voice her doubts. But her sisters would just tell her what she already knew.

"I think Samuel still has a few secrets." It was the easiest way to explain it.

Evie shook her head. "What kind of secrets?"

"I don't know, really." Mattie picked up the spot on her dress where Charlie had eaten the hole. It wasn't like she could just change. She was still waiting on Evie to make her something for church tomorrow. "I mean, I don't know that much about American prisons. But I can imagine that not many good or holy things go on there. An Amish man put in that position." She closed her eyes for a moment. "It doesn't bear thinking."

"So you're saying he can't tell these secrets?" Naomi asked. Her brow crumpled into a frown of confusion, or maybe it was indecision. Mattie wasn't sure. "He'll still have to get up in front of the church and confess all."

"*Jah*, I know," Mattie said. "And I think that's what's bothering him. That he has to talk about that time in his life. It's over now—he is out of that nightmare he was put in. I can't imagine what it's like to have to revisit that, not only in your own thoughts, but in front of all the people you've known your entire life."

"It's not to torture him," Naomi said softly. "It'll be good for him to stand up and say those things. It'll be cleansing to get them out, have them forgiven. He will only be able to let them go once that happens."

Mattie knew this. She had already told herself the same things. And that only left one reason for his reluctance.

And like a fool she had gone and fallen in love with him.

"It may be time to rethink this," Evie said sadly.

"Rethink what?" Mattie asked. Though she knew. She just had to have her sister say it out loud.

"Maybe it's time to rethink marrying him."

Mattie scoffed. "Who said I was going to marry him?"

Naomi and Evie shared a look. Mattie didn't like it one bit. It was that sisters' look, the look of two people who knew you better than you knew yourself.

"It's not the time to be coy," Evie said.

"Coy?" Mattie asked with a small laugh. "Is that one of the words from your romance novels?" *Jah*, she was looking for a diversion. Shine the light on Evie so no one looked at her too closely.

"You don't have to pretend with us," Naomi said. "We know that you've fallen in love with him."

Mattie closed her eyes. She had only just now admitted that to herself. But she wasn't quite ready to admit it to them. "How ridiculous." She gave a scoffing laugh, but knew it wouldn't end here. Her sisters were tenacious if they were anything at all.

They shared another one of those looks, then Naomi turned back and started to speak.

"*Mamm*, more."

They all turned as Gracie toddled into the kitchen. She had the empty cheese wrapper in one hand and a fistful of what could only be squished cheese in the other. Smears of it were already in her dark hair.

Mattie moved toward her daughter. "How in the world did you get out of the high chair?" She asked the question though it in itself was another diversion. She was almost ashamed of herself for taking it. But she didn't have answers to all the questions her sisters were asking. The one answer she did have she wasn't ready to share.

"This is the second time she's escaped. I guess Bethann's been watching me put her in the high chair and she figured out how to get her out of it this morning." Naomi started back into the dining area.

Evie moved to one side to allow everyone free access back and forth.

Mattie picked up Gracie. She avoided Evie's look, and instead opened the refrigerator and got her daughter another snack. Something to tide them over to their delayed dinner.

She pressed her cheek to the side of Gracie's head, planning a quick kiss. "*Danki*, little one. Thank you so much."

Chapter Thirteen

There was only one way to find out the truth, and that was to ask him directly. But the thought made Mattie's stomach clench. How could she ask him that? Not only what he was trying to hide from the congregation, but whether or not he loved her. If he really cared about her enough to face the congregation, stand before the community and ask forgiveness for all that had transpired.

It was the only way, and yet she couldn't bring herself to do it.

So church Sunday passed without incident. Evie had gotten Mattie a new black mourning dress ready for the service and had already started cutting out material for a new everyday one as well.

Mattie couldn't help but notice the stack of white material on the counter next to the sewing machine. She didn't need a new church apron. An everyday apron, *jah*. Those were black.

Besides, it wasn't the right fabric for a church apron. It was more like the material that they used to make men's shirts. The only reason Evie would have yards of that particular white fabric was to make a new shirt for Samuel. A white shirt to wear to church. To repent.

She wanted to believe that Samuel was preparing to stand up in front of the church, to confess all, get right with the church. And it shouldn't be about marrying her. She felt selfish and self-centered in a whole host of emotions that told her she was looking at all of this the wrong way.

Yet she wondered if those emotions were truly leading her in the right direction. Wasn't it something she should let Samuel work out for himself? Or was that just a convenient way for her to not confront him?

Mattie blew on her fingers to warm them up a bit, then she reached into her basket and pulled out another of her girls' dresses. It was Monday. Traditionally a laundry day, time to get everyone's church clothes clean and back in the closet to await the next service, and that next service was Christmas Day.

The year had seemed to fly by quickly. Even those first few weeks after David had passed.

It was Christmas already. Then after that a new year. Gracie's birthday was in the spring. It was hard to believe that her baby was already going to be two.

Somewhere between Christmas and Gracie's birthday, Mattie would have the baby she now carried. Further testament that life went on.

But as far as a wedding, that didn't seem to be happening. Somehow, she had let Samuel convince her to want it on the sheer dream of his word. But as time passed, even just a day, it was one day closer to that not happening.

She would be okay. She didn't need a man in her life. She could handle her responsibilities and her farm. With the help of her sisters. When she needed more help she would turn to a neighbor, hire a handyman. Perhaps even an *Englischer* to come in and do things like repair the metal roof or the fence or to help her find her wayward goat. She could do this. She had the Lord on her side.

Despite the cold wind that blew and the fact that her fingers were frozen from hanging up the wet laundry, Mattie bowed her head and prayed.

Lord, help me do this. You challenged me and put me by myself with only family and friends to help. But I know this is Your plan—this is Your will for me. All I ask is give me the bravery and the fortitude to see it through. Amen.

She opened her eyes and turned back to her laundry. But the dress she just hung was no longer there. She had pinned it up like she was supposed to. She looked to the ground. There stood Charlie, chewing happily on the hem of her new church dress.

"Charlie!" she cried.

She pulled the dress away from the goat, but it was too late.

"What happened?"

She turned as Samuel made his way out of the barn. Her heart gave a hard thump when she saw him, and she recognized it for what it was—that excitement of love. A love that seemed to not be returned. Or at least not enough that he was willing to face his past and the congregation. As much as she hated to admit it, that seemed to be the truth.

"I see," he said, after he spied her dress lying on the ground.

She groaned as she stooped down and tried to wrestle it away from the goat. The beast only pulled back like a dog playing tug-of-war with his master.

"Let go," she commanded. But the goat dug in, a stubborn light shining in her golden eyes.

"Don't scare me like that," Samuel said. "I thought something was really wrong."

Mattie turned back to him, anger flashing

through her. "This is really wrong. She's eating my dress."

"Is the dress savable at this point?"

"No," she grudgingly admitted.

"Then why are you fighting her for it?"

Male logic. Mattie hated it. She let go of the dress and propped her hands on her hips before facing Samuel once more.

"Now you can get it away from her," Mattie said.

"Why would I?"

"Because she doesn't need to be eating it."

"She's a goat."

"No nutritional value," Mattie shot back.

Samuel sighed and went after the goat. She immediately jumped up and ran across the yard, dragging the dress along with her.

Mattie turned back to the laundry, refusing to laugh at the antics of man and goat. She was still upset. She didn't need to be laughing at anything right now. But she couldn't help the smile that twitched on her lips as Samuel cornered the goat next to the water trough, then dove at her in order to grab a hold of the dress. Instead, he fell to the ground facefirst, and Charlie jumped on his back scampering over him, still dragging the dress behind her.

She needed this. She'd just been wondering how she was going to take care of three kids and a mischievous goat, not to mention her herd of milk does. But it seemed even Samuel had trouble with the beast. Maybe she would get through this after all.

Stupid goat. Samuel dusted off the knees of his pants and shook his head.

Stupid man, he corrected. He had wanted to be the hero, to rescue Mattie's dress from that mischievous beast. Instead, he looked like a fool running around, falling in the dirt, being bested by a goat no bigger than most dogs.

Mattie had laughed at him, and he couldn't blame her. He was sure he was a comical sight, outdone by goat. But that was just what love got you.

The only problem was this promise. How was he ever going to prove to her that he loved her for herself? Not because of David, not because of the promise, but because she was a wonderful, caring, loving person who deserved to be loved again.

Even if he didn't.

"Knock, knock."

He turned as Mattie came into the barn, that ornery goat trotting along beside her. He wasn't sure, but he thought he saw a smug look on Charlie's face. He wouldn't put it past the goat at all.

"I'm sorry about your dress," he said.

Mattie shook it off. "I don't know why she's started doing this. Maybe the weather."

He didn't say anything in return. What was there to say? It could be the weather. Or maybe she was just an ill-behaved goat.

Mattie shifted in place. "I didn't come out here to talk about my dress. Or my goat."

Something in her tone was so serious, it took him aback. "What did you come out here to talk about?"

She pulled her shawl a little closer around her shoulders, and he saw that her hands shook with the motion. She was nervous. Why?

"What are your intentions?" she asked.

He cleared his throat. "I told you from the start—"

"You told me you came here to marry me," she cut him short. "And yet you've done nothing to get things in place to make that happen."

"I talked to the bishop—"

"You have to do more than talk." The words were softly spoken, yet they rang around his head like the school bell the teacher used to get them in from recess.

He knew they were true. Just as he knew that he had been dragging his feet. It was just so hard. Faith was one thing. Recovering faith was another. He'd get there, but it was going to take more time than he had originally anticipated. More time than he had if he was going to convince Mattie to marry him.

"You doubt me." He could see it now, what was in her eyes, the hesitancy in her words. He'd come here and said that he was going to marry her because she needed his help. Then he made sure she needed his help, and yet he had done nothing to get the rest of it to happen.

"You don't have to keep that promise," she finally said. Her voice trembled. The mere sound of it made his heart ache. "But I would like to have you around."

Around?

"But you can't stay—" She didn't finish that sentence. She didn't have to. He knew. The bishop would not allow him to stay unless he got himself back right with the church, and he couldn't do that until he got himself back right with himself. And yet as much as he tried to ease all the struggles...

He thought he could fake it. He thought he could come here, say the words, do the actions and carry through with it so that he could fulfill his promise to his brother. But once he was there, he knew he couldn't fake it. How was he supposed to tell her that?

How was he supposed to get back his faith?

"I want to stay around," he said. "I want you to know that."

She nodded, but didn't speak.

"You do know that, right?"

She raised those clear green eyes to his. "Why do you want to be here?"

"This is my home," he said simply. It was the first answer to pop to his head other than the one he wasn't sure he should say yet.

"And that's the only reason?"

She wanted him to say it. He closed his eyes and gathered his courage. "I'm falling in love with you. With all of you. The girls, the farm, your sisters, even your sassy goat."

As he said the words, he could see her visibly relax as the tension left her shoulders. He hadn't noticed before, but she had been clenching her jaw. Now that eased as well. Her lips curved into a smile, a small, tentative smile, hesitant and wondering.

"You're sure?"

"Mattie, why would I tell you that if it weren't the truth?"

"To get me to marry you, because of this promise between you and David."

"Yes, David made me promise something to him. And I came here fully intending on honoring that promise. And I would have, if even on the sole basis that David asked me to take care of his family if something were to happen to him. But then I got here and…" He broke off and shook his head. "I guess I never realized that I missed the valley until I came back." He missed a lot of things. He missed the innocence he had before he left. He missed the good times that they had lived, going to singings and volleyball games and all the other treasures of youth. He knew he couldn't get that back, but somehow, he felt he was one step closer being in Millers Creek. But that didn't have anything to do with falling in love.

"So you want to marry me, because you love my sisters?"

"Mattie…seriously, were you always this stubborn? Do you hear what I'm saying to you? I came here out of obligation and now I'm planning to stay out of love. That's all you need to know."

She walked slowly toward him, her gaze never leaving his. One step and then another until she was right in front of him. She had her arms wrapped around herself in defense of the weather and potential hurts.

"Can I help you?" she asked. "Whatever it is that you need to work through… Can I help you?"

How he wished she could. But this was all on him. "No," he said. "But I appreciate your asking."

"I want you to stay. I—" She paused. "I think I'm falling in love with you too."

As far as declarations of love went, it was half-hearted at best, but it still made his heart soar. Maybe now she was getting a love for him mixed up with grief for her husband, but once they were married, once they had really begun a life together, he hoped she could somehow compartmentalize her time with his brother away from her time with him. Only years together would smooth that out. But even without a promise, this was what he would want. Her, loving him in any way.

"That's all I can ask for," he finally said. He wanted to reach over, pull her closer and kiss her like he had before. There were no magical stars above. This time he couldn't blame it on the night. Not standing here in broad daylight in the barn with a goat nipping at his shoelaces. It was all too real and out in the open.

Instead, he tugged on her arms and pulled her hands out. He clasped them in his own. "After the New Year," he started, "I'll bend my knee. I'll confess my sins, my transgressions, everything to the church. I'll make things right. After that we can talk about getting married. Maybe even by this time next year."

She gave him a trembling smile. "I'd like that."

Something within him melted at her words. It gave him a joy like he hadn't felt in a long, long time. He knew then he would do whatever it took to keep her smiling like that. "First church service next year. I promise."

The week leading up to Christmas was a joyous one. Mattie was looking forward to having church on Christmas Day and wished that Samuel could join them. But even with his uncle as the deacon, it wouldn't be allowed.

She finished Samuel's scarf and wrapped it in pretty red paper covered with white snowflakes. She had to forgo bows this year. It seemed that Charlie had switched her preference for eating Mattie's dresses to eating the bows off the presents. And after a particularly gross encounter with curling ribbon, Mattie declared all bows banned from the house until further notice.

Mattie rode to church with a smile on her face the entire way. It wasn't just Christmas though. Samuel had claimed that he was falling in love with her. What more could she ask for as a Christmas gift? She was being given a second chance at love. It was beautiful, and she was thankful, even though she knew she was not worthy.

Samuel had promised that the next church

service would be the service that would start the reversal of his excommunication. And this time he had promised. He used those words, *I promise*.

In the meantime, they would go about their lives, not acting on the building love between them. Yet confident and content in the fact that it existed between them.

There was no surprise that the preacher spoke of Mary and Joseph during the sermon, of their trials, trust in each other, standing side by side through what had to be a most difficult time. They had come through all of that to raise a savior. *The* savior. And suddenly any trial she had faced seemed so small.

She wasn't the only one who left the service with tears in her eyes.

As usual, she helped the women serve the meal, then grabbed a plate for herself and her girls, locating a seat just inside the barn.

"It's snowing!" someone called.

Mattie couldn't see the outside from where she sat, but it was magical all the same, snow on Christmas Day. Suddenly, she just wanted to be at home. She wanted to open gifts then have a small dinner since it was Sunday. Cooking a large meal was out of the question today. Sunday was a day of rest. But tomorrow...tomorrow she had promised to bake a ham. And though it would break the rules of his shunning, she had vowed to invite Samuel in to eat.

It was one thing to eat by yourself when no one was celebrating, and quite another to sit mere yards away from where others held a Christmas feast. It just didn't seem right. But she could only get in trouble for that if the bishop found out, and no one who she knew was about to tell him.

"Eat up, girls," she said. She scraped the last bite from her plate and started toward the trash can. She glanced back at her girls happily eating side by side. They made her think so much of her and her own sisters with their different coloring and different personalities, and yet they loved each other so very much. It was all she could hope for. And this new baby, boy or girl, she welcomed them with open arms and prayed that they had the same relationship as Gracie and Bethann.

"Mattie," a voice said behind her. "There you are."

Mattie turned to see Eleanor Peachey approaching, a large lavender-colored envelope in one hand.

"Here I am," Mattie said. "But I need to get back to my girls." She gestured to where her daughters sat on the converted church pews.

They were getting along for now, but who

knew how long that would last. It was better to be close by just in case.

"*Jah*, sure," Eleanor said. "I'll just follow along. This is important."

Something in her tone had the joy draining from Mattie's happy disposition. It was Christmas Day; what in a purple envelope could be that important on Christmas Day?

Thankfully, the girls were finished eating and even more thankfully, Gracie managed to get some of it in her mouth and not all of it in her hair.

Mattie opened her bag and got out a wet wipe. She handed one to Bethann who could handle the task herself and grabbed another for Gracie. She proceeded to clean most of the mess off Gracie in preparation to leave. She wanted to get home. She wanted to see Samuel. She wanted to open Christmas gifts with her family and watch it snow outside. It was a magical day to be sure.

"I have that friend, you remember?" Eleanor said.

"A friend?" What friend was she talking about?

"My friend Becky in western Pennsylvania. I finally heard back from her and—" Eleanor shook her head. She pressed her lips together in that disapproving way she had.

"What?" Her heart started to sink; her stomach clenched tighter and tighter until it neared pain. Eleanor had a flair for the dramatic, she reminded herself. This could be nothing. Or it could be something. Something big enough that Eleanor sought Mattie out so she could tell her before she left. It was hard to know. So Mattie waited patiently for Eleanor to finish her dramatic pause and continue.

"I wrote her a letter, see," Eleanor finally said. "About Samuel. I told you something wasn't right. He lived with the *Englisch*. That's why he wasn't right with the church."

The tension eased out of Mattie shoulders. "I know this. He had to go to prison." It was next to impossible to be Amish in prison. All the things that were required of a body to do, go to church, be a part of the community. A person might be able to pray or even uphold their values in that situation, but it wasn't possible to keep a standing in the church. It just wasn't. She understood that. Surely Eleanor understood that as well.

"No," Eleanor said with a shake of her head. "He was working with this *Englisch* contractor before that. That's when he got in trouble and had to go to prison."

"*Jah,*" Mattie said as patiently as possible. She started packing up the girls, getting them ready to get back into the buggy. Coats on, scarves wrapped around their heads. As soon as she got them ready, she was going to find her sisters and leave. It was time to go home. And somehow, now, in this conversation with Eleanor, she felt like it was past time to leave.

"You miss my point. He was living *Englisch* before that. He was even married and had a baby."

The words took Mattie's breath away. "Who said he had a baby?" It wasn't possible. It had to be a mistake. He would've told her. If he had been married and had an *Englisch* wife and an *Englisch* baby, where were they now?

Eleanor held up the lavender envelope. "It's all right here." She took the letter out and handed it to Mattie.

A wave of nausea rose over Mattie, and she swallowed hard. Fortunately, she hadn't been ill with this baby, hadn't had a lot of sickness, but this was something else entirely. As if the baby knew, it kicked her in the side.

Mattie winced and rubbed the spot with one hand while she held the letter with the other. She scanned it as quickly as possible until she found the part about Samuel. She read it once, twice, and one more time just to make sure she read all the words correctly.

Samuel had gone out to New Wilmington. He

had stayed with their church for a small time, then left. He never returned. He was put under the *Bann*. Then rumor got around that he had married a woman and had a baby. An *Englisch* woman. Then there was the trouble with the contractor, the charges of embezzlement and fraud and a prison sentence. But that was all. Nothing about where that wife and baby were now.

Mattie took a deep breath, blew it out, then refolded the letter and handed it back to Eleanor. "I appreciate the information," she said as calmly as possible, even though her heart was breaking in two. How could he have come and told her that he was going to marry her when he was married to another?

"I thought you should know. I hear that you two are getting very close." Eleanor searched her face for some clue to her feelings; Mattie did her best to school her expression into an unreadable mask of indifference. Polite indifference.

"He's family," Mattie reminded her.

"Jah, jah," Eleanor said with a vigorous nod. "Of course he is, dear. But I just thought you should know."

It took everything in Mattie's power not to turn the woman around and point her in the opposite direction and tell her to go. Instead, she smiled, grabbed up the girls and once again thanked the woman for showing her the letter and breaking her heart. Though, she left that last part unsaid.

She found Evie and Naomi talking with their other sisters about having dinner the following evening. Mattie had already committed to making a ham, and now it seemed she was committed to making a ham and taking it to her father's house. It was not what she wanted. She wanted to spend it with Samuel. And now...

And now how could she?

"It's time to go," Mattie said, sending Naomi and Evie urgent looks. She had to get out of there before she broke down.

"Okay, let me get my coat," Evie said.

Naomi continued to chatter away with her twin, Priscilla.

No, she could keep it together. She had to keep it together. Besides, she didn't even know if what the woman said was true. She didn't know this Becky woman from Adam. What if she was just making stuff up?

And why would she do that?

Mattie shook her head. Why did anybody do anything?

Why did Samuel come back proposing marriage and rebuilding a family when he already had a family tucked away somewhere? Unless...

"Can we go now?"

Naomi eyed her in confusion. "Evie?"

"Right," Mattie said. She shifted Gracie on her hip. Her back was beginning to ache from the extra weight of the baby she carried and the baby in her arms. Though Gracie was getting too big to call a baby these days.

"Here." Naomi held her arms out to Gracie. "Let me have her."

Mattie turned her toddler over to her sister and immediately felt the ease on her back muscles. Though they still ached, mostly with tension. But she would get to the bottom of this. Somehow, she would find out the truth. And maybe the truth wasn't as bad as it seemed right in that moment. Maybe it was only part of the truth. She didn't need to jump to conclusions until she had a chance to talk to Samuel himself.

"I'm ready," Evie said, shuffling over to them.

"Let's go." Mattie grabbed Bethann's hand once again and steered her toward the door.

They had to say their farewells and merry Christmases to a few members of their congregation as they made their way out of the barn and into the snow.

Bethann stopped four times on the way to the buggy to throw her head back, open her mouth and stick out her tongue to catch snowflakes. Any other time, Mattie would have laughed at her sweet childish antics. But not today. It was

Christmas, and yet it held the foreboding of disaster.

"What's wrong?" Naomi asked as they waited for the young man to retrieve their horse from the pasture.

"Something Eleanor said," Mattie replied. As far as answers went it wasn't very explanatory, but there were too many little ears around.

"Eleanor's full of hot—" Naomi started.

"Air," Evie finished.

Naomi frowned at her sister. "That's what I was going to say."

"Sometimes I wonder," Evie replied.

Naomi rolled her eyes. Then she turned her attention to Mattie. "You shouldn't believe everything Eleanor tells you."

"I don't," Mattie said. "But I need to get home so I can find out."

"So it's about Samuel then," Evie guessed.

Naomi moved away to get the horse and hitch it to their buggy. It was only a few minutes later that they were on the road home. The closer they got to the house, the more nervous Mattie became.

What if what Eleanor said was true?

How was she supposed to go in there and talk to Samuel about these things? Just how did one ask their brother-in-law what happened to his wife and child? Because either something happened to them, or they were somewhere else. And even if they were divorced, even if they had split up in the *Englisch* world, according to the Amish church, they were still married. The church didn't recognize divorce; marriage was till death do you part. And unless his wife had passed on…

Mattie reined in her thoughts. It was like a dog chasing its tail. Worrying her and worrying her when the answer would come in a few moments. Just as soon as she got the girls unloaded from the buggy and went out to the barn. Hopefully Samuel was around somewhere and hadn't gone back to camp. Surely he would be coming up soon anyway. Christmas or no, the goats had to be milked. There was no getting out of that one.

As they climbed down from the buggy, the snow really begin to fall. It fell across the land like a blanket of quiet beauty. Why was a white Christmas so special? She didn't know. It just was. And now this Christmas…

She turned to Naomi. "Can you take the girls inside?"

Her sister nodded.

"I'll take care of the horse." She unhooked the mare and headed for the barn.

Her heart beat triple time in her chest as she entered. The snow outside seemed to make everything a little bit brighter and a hush had fallen over the animals. She could hear the goats next door bleating and calling to one another. But the horse was quiet and the barn silent.

She led the mare into the stall, then went back to the tack room for the brush. She needed something to do with her hands. Something calming.

She was a coward. She couldn't imagine that Samuel was back in his tent, not with the snow coming down like this. He was around here somewhere. And she'd been as silent as possible as she came in. She could've called out to him at any time but she hadn't.

"Mattie," Samuel greeted as he came down from the loft. "I thought I heard someone down here. How was church?"

How was church?

Mattie left the stall and went to get the scoop of the horse feed for Bessie. "Fine," she replied.

"Good, good," he said.

Her heart was filled with love for this man. But was he really who he said he was? She supposed that had been the question all along. Samuel had gone away for an extended amount of time. Now no one truly knew who he was, the person he had become in his time away. A married person? A father?

"What's wrong?" he asked. Her silence must've tipped him off.

Mattie set the brush on a nearby hay bale and turned to face him. "It seems Eleanor Peachey has a friend out in western Pennsylvania."

His eyes were filled with innocence and confusion as he waited for her to continue.

"This friend wrote her a letter and told her some things about you." She stopped then. How did one ask another person if they had led a secret life? If they'd been lying all along? "She said you had a wife and a child. Is that true?"

She asked that last little question, but she could see the answer on his face. His expression was a hybrid of horror and sadness and regret.

"So it's true," she said calmly. She amazed herself that she could remain steady through this. Perhaps she had known all along that something wasn't right. Perhaps she had just been waiting for this moment so it could all come crashing down.

"It's not what you think," Samuel said.

"Oh, it's what I think all right," she said with a derisive laugh. Even to her own ears the sound rang forced and untrue. "You left here, and you went out there. Then you left the church, found a wife, had a baby. I thought you were living an *Englisch* life in prison, not before prison."

"I never said that."

Mattie shook her head. She was growing numb to the pain of the heartbreak she was now facing. It must be some defense mechanism. She was already in mourning, already grieving for her husband, pregnant and trying to figure out what she was going to do in this life without the man she once loved, and now this. It was simply too much. "No, you never did. But you allowed me to believe it."

"I didn't mean to deceive you." He took a step toward her.

Mattie held out one hand to stop him. "Don't." She didn't want him anywhere near her. It was hard enough to think without adding his warmth and closeness to the mix. "Where are they?"

"Who?"

"Don't do this to me, Samuel. You and I have both been through too much for you to start playing games now." Though he had been playing games all along, hadn't he?

"They're dead."

Mattie's breath caught in her throat. Dead.

Tears filled Samuel's eyes. She wanted to believe they were fake tears, crocodile tears, but she knew they were real. He had loved and lost; she had loved and lost. She knew that pain. He had not only lost a spouse, but a child as well. She put her hand over her belly protectively.

"It's hard for me to talk about," he said.

"You came here saying right from the start that you were gonna marry me. You should be able to tell me anything. Isn't that what marriage is all about?"

"To be fair," he started, "I came here to marry you, *jah*. But I wasn't in love with you when I came here. By the time I fell in love with you, it seemed, I don't know, too late to start spouting off secrets. Not only am I in bad standing with the church, but I killed my wife and child."

Chapter Fourteen

The horrified look on her face shamed him. But that was what he had been going for, wasn't it? To show her just how bad the world was. How bad *he* was?

She shook her head, her own tears running down her cheeks. "I don't believe that," she said. But there was a look in her eyes, just the edge of doubt in this trust, a gap between them, the years he had lived away from the church.

"It's true." It was actually a relief to say so. He'd been carrying the burden around with him for a year to be exact.

"What happened?"

He didn't want to go down that road. He shook his head.

"You can't do that," she said. "You can't say something like that and not explain. That's not fair, Samuel."

"Tell me something that is fair, Mattie?" He didn't need to say the rest to her, that she was pregnant and widowed, living on her own, trying to run a farm when her husband had had a freak accident. Otherwise he would be alive right then to share it all with her.

"I invited you in," she said. "You are under a *Bann*, and I invited you in as much as I possibly could. I tried to help you. I've defended you. The least you can do now is tell me the truth."

The truth.

Samuel braced his hands on his hips and expelled a long breath. "What difference does it make?" It wouldn't make any difference in the long run if she knew how Emma and Sadie had died.

But the look on her face.

"When I was sentenced," he finally said, "they moved me about a hundred miles away, and Emma, my wife, wanted to come visit. I told her not to. But she insisted. On the way she was in a car accident. Apparently, a man driving the other way on the highway had a heart attack, crossed the median and hit them head-on. Everyone died."

She bit her lips and shook her head, the tears still coming. "I don't see how that's your fault," she said.

"If I hadn't been in prison, she wouldn't have

been traveling that road. I'm as responsible as if I'd been driving the other car myself."

"That's not how it works."

He felt that familiar rage, white-hot and blistering, rise up within him. He gritted his teeth and his eyes met hers. "That's how I feel."

It took him a moment to get himself back together, and she allowed him the time. For that, he was grateful. There was something different in her eyes now. She would never look at him the same way. One of the reasons why he hadn't told her.

"You lied to me."

The words fell like a bomb between them. It shattered everything and left an eerie calm in its place. It shook the very ground they stood on. He knew for certain, things would never be the same again. "I… I just didn't tell you about them."

"A lie of omission is still a lie. I know your mother taught you that."

"Mattie," he started, though he had no idea what he was going to follow up with. *I'm sorry? Forgive me? Don't walk out of here?* But none of those words came.

She pushed past him and toward the door of the barn. "It's Christmas," she said simply, coldly. "But I expect you to be out of here tomorrow."

* * *

Mattie walked stiffly across the yard, the falling snow swirling around her. It was beginning to fall faster and thicker than it had been before. There would be inches on the ground before dark. A beautiful white Christmas. And it was all ruined.

He had ruined it with his lies. How could she forgive him that? She had told him anything could happen to anybody. She had understood and he was still noble in her eyes, but a wife and a child? An *Englisch* wife and the *Englisch* child? He never once mentioned them in the weeks that he had been there. And he claimed to love her. How could a person love someone and keep something like that from them? They couldn't, she decided. It was impossible. For when one person truly loved another, they wanted to share everything with them. He knew about David; she had told him the trials they had gone through, what they had done to get the farm started. How he had died. How she missed him. That she had wondered how she was going to raise this baby without him. This baby and his girls.

There were so many signs, she thought as she grabbed a handrail and made her way slowly up the porch steps. They were slick and she was shaking. She didn't want to fall.

So many signs, she thought as she grabbed the door handle and let herself into the house. She stopped on the rug just inside the door, shivering from the cold and the news that had been delivered to her.

She couldn't say for certain, didn't really want to think about it, but would she be upset if he had told her about a wife and a child now gone? Once loved. Always remembered.

No, she wouldn't be upset if he had told her. She could've understood that. They could have worked around it. She wouldn't have been caught off guard. But a wife and a child...

"So it's true," Evie said, coming in from the kitchen.

Mattie had been so engrossed in her own thoughts, she hadn't even heard the clank of her sister's crutches as she approached.

The tears that had fallen silently in the barn became sobs as her sister approached.

Mattie put her arms around Evie and drew her close. She was thankful that she had told her sisters the news in the carriage, spelling most of the words so the girls wouldn't understand. It had been difficult to reveal all that, but now she was grateful that she had swallowed whatever despair she felt then and let them know. For now, she wouldn't have to say much more about the situation. Except...

"They're dead," she managed between sobs. "He said they died in a car crash."

Naomi come bustling down the stairs. "I thought I heard the door—" She took one look at the sisters and rushed over to them, wrapping her arms around each one of them as well. A sisters' hug.

"So it's true," Naomi said. "He has a family."

"They've passed," Evie said simply.

Mattie was thankful for her sisters' words, for she couldn't find her own. She was doing everything in her power to swallow back sobs to get herself together once more.

It was Christmas, and they had gifts to open. But now everything seemed ruined.

Yet it couldn't be. She had children to take care of and things to do, other people who wanted to enjoy this day and not have to wallow in her sadness.

She let go of her sisters and stepped back, her shoulders hitting the door in the process. "I'm okay. I'm okay," she said even as she willed it to be so. She wiped the tears away on the tail of her apron, only then realizing she was still in her church clothes, and this was her church apron she'd just wiped tears on. Thankfully it didn't leave a streak.

"Where are the girls?"

Naomi waved in the direction of the staircase. "Up in their room. I have them changing clothes."

Mattie winced. "Together?" Was it just a day for disaster?

Naomi gave a small almost apologetic shrug. "Bethann said she wanted to help her sister. We were talking about how she's going to be the oldest of three pretty soon, and she'll have to take on more and more responsibility."

Mattie shook her head and gave her sister a wide, though watery, smile. "*Jah*, that's the way you do it. Push it all off on the oldest."

"I do what I can," Naomi said.

"And where's my goat?"

Again Naomi gave that negligent wave toward the staircase. "With the girls."

"And they're changing clothes?" Mattie said just to be sure.

"*Jah.*"

"So the goat who wants to eat dresses is upstairs with them and everyone is unsupervised."

Naomi's eyes grew wide. She reached up to straighten her prayer *kapp*, then turned on her heel and headed back for the stairs.

Evie and Mattie were still standing by the door when they heard Naomi shout, "Oh, Charlie!"

Evie looked back at Mattie and smiled. "I

guess it's a good thing I bought some extra fabric when I was in town the other day."

Mattie smiled, doing her best to piece the broken shards of her heart back together, for their sake, for everyone's sake. "I guess it's a good thing you like to sew."

Once the girls were changed and the dresses put aside for playtime, after a good patching of course, everyone came downstairs to open gifts.

Mattie kept reminding herself that today was a blessing. A church Sunday. A Christmas Sunday. Never mind bad news and broken hearts. This was about her family and her children. Tomorrow they were going to her father's house. She would take the ham, and they would eat together and be joyous together and celebrate together. But for now, like a typical Sunday, they would eat cold meat, cheese, and crackers, maybe even with some peanut butter spread, for supper. The girls would play with their crayons and modeling clay and other toys that they had gotten from their aunts and their mother.

But even as the night wound down and the snow continued to fall, all Mattie could think about was Samuel. It didn't help that his present was sitting right across from her on the table by the window. One of three presents left there by her and her sisters. Aside from the scarf that

Mattie had knitted, a thick black woolly thing designed to keep whoever wore it as warm as possible in a Pennsylvania winter, Naomi had made him a pan of strawberry cupcakes, and Evie had made him a church shirt.

Mattie sometimes sat in wonder of her sisters' generosity. Evie had such a big, loving heart. But there were so many people around who despite their upbringing could only see Evie for her disability and not the things that she could offer. The thought saddened Mattie even more than she already was. But she wasn't going to let heartbreak ruin her night.

"*Mamm!* I want cookies!"

Mattie turned around to find her two girls standing on the bottom step, looking as innocent as angels on this beautiful Christmas night.

"Is that how you ask for something?" Mattie quizzed in return. One little snack before bed. And then they would all turn in and see what tomorrow held.

"Peas." Bethann grinned broadly, obviously proud of herself for remembering.

"Come on," Naomi called from the kitchen doorway. She had a tray of glasses in one hand and a tray of cookies in the other. Behind her, Evie toted the milk.

Mattie smiled. Everyone was going to have one little snack before bed on this beautiful

Christmas night. She made her way over to the table where everyone had gathered around.

She offered, but Naomi refused to let her pour the milk. Evie dished out everyone two of the delicious sugar cookies that the girls and their aunt had decorated the day before. Stars and angels and even just plain round ones with beautiful colored icing and sugar sprinkles.

Mattie did her best to forget all about her troubles and to live in that one moment. It would never happen again. It would never be this Christmas again. Her daughters would never again be this age. Who knew what the New Year would bring them. She had learned this year that shocking news could happen in an instant. She needed to savor this.

"I make." Bethann held up a cookie and grinned proudly.

"I can see that," Mattie said. Mainly because it had about half an inch of icing on the top. She shouldn't let her kids eat this much sugar before bed, but only on Christmas. And then tomorrow... Well, they would have to see what tomorrow would bring when tomorrow came.

Christmas or not, he had outstayed his welcome. And he had failed. His brother had made him promise and he had failed to fulfill his twin's wishes.

Samuel gathered what he had in Mattie's barn and headed out. The snow was thick, coming down in huge flakes that stuck to everything. But the magic of a white Christmas was gone.

He had messed up in not talking to Mattie more about Emma and Sadie. But it was so hard to even let their names into his thoughts. Mattie wasn't the only one who he had failed, and despite what she said, he couldn't talk himself out of feeling responsible for their deaths. Maybe if he had stood up and fought more in court. Maybe if he hadn't let his Amish side dictate his response to the charges against him.

Maybe, maybe, maybe. What if, what if, what if.

None of that mattered now. It was over and done. He only could hope and pray that those he had wronged would forgive him. Someday.

He trudged through the snow, back to the place where he had camped. But his tent was gone. At least it was gone from sight. The snow was so heavy that it had broken it down and everything was flat. He couldn't stay there. He didn't even know if he could get his tent back up right from the inside, and the snow was coming down fast.

He looked toward Mattie's house, then in the direction of his mother's. Would she let him in, even on a night like tonight? He wasn't sure.

And he was freezing. His feet were starting to go numb in his boots and his nose was so cold it was beginning to run. He needed to get out of this weather.

Perhaps Martha...

It was a chance he was taking in heading for his sister's. Her husband wasn't exactly supportive of Samuel's life decisions. Joshua Glick could just as easily turn Samuel away as his mother. But if there was one person who would stand up for him, it was Martha.

It was a longer walk from his camp to Martha's house, and his boots were caked with snow by the time he made it there. The snow that was falling soaked into his coat. The bottom of his pants from about the knee down was wet. The chill had set in and his teeth were chattering. His hand shook as he raised it to knock on his sister's door.

He saw movement at the window, then the door was wrenched open. "Samuel!" Martha exclaimed. "Get in here." She grabbed hold of his elbow and dragged him into the house.

"Can I stay in your barn?" His teeth were chattering so bad now that he could hardly be understood.

Yet somehow Martha knew. "No," she said with a frown. "Nobody can stay in the barn right now. It's too cold."

"My—my tent collapsed," he explained.

At that moment Joshua Glick, his sister's husband, came out of the kitchen carrying a big glass of milk and a cookie. He stopped in his tracks when he saw Samuel standing there.

He turned to his wife. "Martha?" Just the sound of her name was like she was being chastised.

But she wasn't listening. "Take off your boots, Samuel. And come over here by the fire. You'll freeze to death if we don't get you dry."

"Thank you," he said as she steered him by the elbow toward the warm crackling fire.

"Martha," Joshua said again.

"Not now," she told him sternly. "Not yet." She disappeared down the hallway.

Samuel reached his hands toward the warmth of the fire while Joshua stood in place and watched. It seemed to take forever before Martha reappeared, carrying two towels. She handed him one, then bustled over and placed the other on the puddle forming under his boots.

"Danki," Samuel said. His teeth finally began to not chatter as bad.

"Martha," Joshua said.

His sister looked from Samuel to her husband, then shooed him toward the kitchen. "In here."

As Samuel warmed himself by the fire, as he

started to get circulation back into his fingers and toes, and his nose began to thaw, he heard them talking. He couldn't make out any words, but the tones were obvious. Joshua did not want him in the house, and Martha was not backing down.

It wasn't that Joshua was a bad person; he was a rule follower. The rule was Samuel was shunned.

He should leave. Before he caused them any sort of marital strife. His sister was a good person. Joshua was a good person. He shouldn't put them in this situation. He would get his boots back on and head over to his mother's house. With any luck, he could sneak into the barn and remain there overnight. Then when the snow stopped, he could see what he could make out of his camp.

Samuel put his hands close to the fire one more time, then headed back toward the door, where his boots rested.

"What are you doing?"

He turned from shoving his foot into his boot to face his sister. "I shouldn't have come here. I just wanted to stay in the barn. I don't want to cause you any problems."

"You're not causing us any problems," Martha said. "Is he, Joshua?"

Samuel knew that tone well; she was daring her husband to defy her on this one.

"No," Joshua said.

But Samuel could tell the man wasn't happy about it. "I'll be fine," he said. "In the barn, if I can. If not…" He didn't finish. If not, he would head to his mother's and sleep in her barn. They could work out everything else in the morning.

"No," she said. "You'll stay here. You can sleep in the spare room. There's a bed in there. You'll be warm."

He was grateful. So very grateful.

"Now take off those boots and follow me." Martha turned and started up the staircase. But she stopped and threw a quick glance over her shoulder to her husband. "Start some water for coffee, please."

Samuel gave a quick nod to Joshua as he walked by. He didn't want to be overly gracious. He wouldn't want the man to have any reason to change his mind. Though with the look on Martha's face, that probably wasn't possible.

"I really appreciate this, Martha. I really don't want to cause any problems though."

She shook her head, then opened the door at the top of the staircase, just off to the left. "With the weather outside tonight, I think the bishop will understand."

"Jah" was all he could manage.

She crossed the room and lit the lantern on the opposite side next to a twin bed. The room was filled with this and that, boxes and what appeared to be furniture that had no other place in the house.

"I'll get you something dry to put on," she said.

"Don't go to all that trouble," he protested. "I'll be dry in no time." He hung his coat on the back of a nearby chair and laid his hat on top of one of the miscellaneous boxes scattered around. His socks were wet and the bottom of his pants was soaked, but other than that he was pretty good, all things considered.

She shook her head in that obstinate way that was all Martha. "You'll catch pneumonia. I'll be right back."

Samuel had never felt so intrusive in his life. Not even when he went to Mattie's farm and demanded that she let him muck out the stalls. He perched on the edge of the bed and waited for his sister to come back. He peeled off his wet socks and hung them over the footboard to dry.

"These are Joshua's. You can sleep in this tonight and by morning your own clothes should be dry enough." She handed him a soft T-shirt and a pair of flannel pajama pants. "There's an extra blanket in the closet if you get cold."

She turned as if to leave, but he caught her hand and stopped her.

"Martha," he said quietly. He waited until she

looked at him before he continued. "I really do appreciate this."

He didn't have to say it, but he really appreciated her sticking her neck out for him, her going toe-to-toe with her husband to help him, and he really appreciated the fact that she overlooked his standing with the church in his time of need.

"I know. You're my brother. I love you, but it's time."

As much as he knew she was right, he could not nod in agreement. Yes, it was time, and yet he still wasn't ready.

His silence must've been telling, for she continued. "You've been here weeks now, Samuel. You've had three church services to come forward. Why haven't you? What is keeping you from getting right with the church?"

What was it? How did he explain? "God's will," he finally said.

She frowned. "Are you saying you're not getting right with the church as part of God's will?"

He shook his head. "I just don't see it anymore. It was so clear when we were younger and we accepted things because they happened and it was God's will, but now, I see things and I think I could've prevented that. If this had not happened or that had not happened."

"You've got it all wrong."

"I was married." It was getting easier to say the words.

She drew in a sharp breath. "You were married?"

"We had a baby. A little girl. Sadie."

A small smile trembled on her lips. "I had a niece?"

"Poor thing." He gave a little chuckle. "Looked just like me."

"But you talk about them in the past tense." It wasn't a question, yet it deserved an answer.

"Yes," he said. "They're dead. And if I hadn't been in prison, they would still be alive."

She shook her head. "You don't know that, Samuel. There's no way in the world you could know that."

"Okay, and that would mean it was God's will. Why would God will something like that? Why would He allow them to die? And David? What about him?

"I'm sure everyone in town knows I went to prison. What you don't know is I didn't fight the charges. I took a plea deal so I could get a shorter sentence. That way I could be back with my wife and child as quickly as possible. They moved me about an hour away and she was coming to see me. That's when she got in a car wreck. If I hadn't been in prison, then she wouldn't have died."

Martha moved to sit next to him on the bed. She grabbed one of his hands in hers and held his cold fingers in her warm ones. "What you don't know is if you hadn't been in prison, would the same thing have happened on a different day, on a different road, at a different time?"

He frowned. "God's will."

"We never know why things happen, but for us God's will is a comfort." She looked around her at the room where they sat. "I wanted to turn this room into a nursery."

"Why don't you?"

She smiled a bit sadly. "Because there is no baby. And sometimes I feel like there's probably not ever going to be a baby for me. But I'm making peace with it. I have to. Or it will drive me over the edge."

"Are you saying I'm already there?" He squeezed her fingers playfully.

"No," she replied. "But I do think you're gonna make yourself that way if you keep going over all the what-ifs and the maybes and the alternatives that could've happened. What happened has happened, and you can't go back. Oh, there are days when I wish I could go back," she said. Her face got a faraway look, and Samuel realized how much of her life he'd missed. "But there's only forward. And if you want to remain here in Millers Creek—"

"I do."

"—Then forward is kneeling before the church. Forward is making things right. You may always have doubts. And you may always have to stop yourself from wondering and mulling over all the what-ifs and maybes, but it's not wallowing in them that makes all the difference." She blinked back the tears in her eyes, squeezed his hand one last time, then stood. "I'll see you in the morning."

She closed the door behind her, leaving Samuel alone with his thoughts and her words.

He knew she was right. Everything she said rang true. What was a man to do? A man was supposed to take care of his family, and he hadn't taken care of his. He hadn't been there for them. How could he forgive himself that? How could he accept it as God's will?

The words filled his head as if from above.

It wasn't that God willed people to die, but that He had a plan for them afterward. And Samuel's plan was here in Millers Creek. With Mattie. If he hadn't already ruined that.

He most likely had. He hadn't meant to lie to her; he hadn't meant to deceive her. He surely hadn't meant to hurt her. But he was hurting himself, working through the loss still after a year of Emma and Sadie being gone. Mattie should understand that, having just lost David.

And yes, he was quick in trying to build something back, but there was God's plan again, right before them, just waiting for them to complete it.

Yet there was one thing he had to do before he did anything else at all.

Samuel got down on his knees and prayed.

Chapter Fifteen

The snow blanketed everything for two or three days before it was clear enough to get out and do things. Not that Mattie felt like doing much at all. Her heart was broken. But it was slowly being patched back together by the love of her sisters and her daughters. *Jah*, and her sassy little goat.

But on a dairy farm, work didn't stop for the weather. Or broken hearts. The goats needed to be milked and the cheese needed to be made and the store needed to be manned for those brave souls who did manage to get out with all the snow on the ground to come buy the goats' milk and chèvre.

It was good to stay busy. Good for the body, and for the soul. With work at hand, it kept her from thinking too much about all the lies that Samuel had told her. Because the more she thought about it, the more her heart softened.

She would forgive him, *jah*. She was Amish.

That was part of their community, forgiveness and love for one another. But that didn't mean she had to forget it happened. And she wouldn't. He had deceived her. He had withheld truth from her, and in the end, he had broken her heart. Every night she prayed that he would find whatever peace he needed to make it right with God and the church.

If he stayed in Millers Creek, she would see him on a regular basis. Somehow, she would get through that. But she knew he needed to stay in Millers Creek. The world outside was a big and evil place. Their preacher and deacon talked about it often on Sundays. As did the minister and the bishop. There were too many temptations in the world. Too many distractions to lead a person astray, to lead a person away from God. And the only hope that Samuel had was to stay in Millers Creek, no matter the pain it would cause her.

Still, she couldn't help but wonder why he had come claiming a promise from David and saying that he was going to marry her. Could she believe any of that? He had told her so many half-truths, what made her believe that this one was the truth?

She supposed he just felt guilty for his own shortcomings. That he felt he had somehow failed his wife and his daughter and he would make that up with her. Well, she wasn't going to be the end of the pity promise. He would have to find his forgiveness with the Lord just like the rest of them.

She heard the rattle of a buggy and stepped out of the barn. The cold hit her quick and fast. Though the temperature was frigid, the snow was melting as the sun shone down from the bright blue sky. She turned to see Freeman Yoder driving his buggy down the lane.

She raised one hand to her forehead to shield her eyes from the glare. *Jah*, it was Freeman Yoder. She supposed he had come to see Evie.

Though she vehemently denied it, Mattie suspected that Evie was in love with Freeman. But Freeman was engaged to marry Helen Schrock. Once that happened, the three mutual friends would never be the same. Mattie hated that for her sister. Just as much as she hated that her heart would be broken with unrequited love.

Mattie waited until Freeman set the brake on his carriage and hopped down before greeting him. "Hi," she said. "Evie's in the house."

Freeman reached into the buggy and pulled out a black straw hat. Not his hat, that one was still on his head. "I didn't come to see Evie," he said. "I mean, I would love to go see Evie in a minute, but I really came to give this to you."

"What is it?" she asked though she knew.

"David's hat. I've been meaning to give it to you, but the time never seemed right and now…

Well, I think you should have it." He held the hat out to her.

Mattie took it, fingers trembling as she held the familiar item in her hands. *"Danki,"* she said.

She wasn't going to cry. David was gone, and she had the hat that he had been wearing when he fell into the manure pit at the Yoders' house.

It'd been a freak accident, him falling. He wasn't being unsafe. The doctor suggested, after hearing the descriptions of his fall, that perhaps he had a drop in blood sugar or blood pressure that caused a dizzy spell. At the time she hadn't thought much about the doctor's explanation but now, holding his hat in her hands, she remembered the doctor's appointment he had made for the week after he died. He had been complaining about his vision for a couple of weeks before Mattie convinced him to make an appointment. But he told the doctor it wasn't serious, that there was no hurry. An appointment was made a few weeks out. In between that time, he fell into the pit and died.

"I'm sorry," Freeman was saying. "I didn't mean to…"

She shook her head and gave him a sad smile. "No," she said. "I'm glad to have it. *Danki*, Freeman."

He gave her a small, relieved smile and tipped his own hat toward her. "I'll go see Evie now."

Mattie stood in the yard, her muck boots sinking in the mud as she held David's precious hat in her hands.

It was time to let go.

As if in agreement, the baby kicked and tumbled inside her. She pressed a hand to her belly and smiled.

"That's right, little one."

Next week—no, tomorrow. Tomorrow she would start to gather his clothes and give them away. There were plenty of people in their community who needed the things that he'd had. There was no sense hanging on to them. She had all these memories. She had two children from him, hopefully a third arriving soon. He would live on in his kids, his daughters and his unborn child. Yes, tomorrow.

He was the boy who cried wolf. The one who said the wolf was coming to gain attention when there was no wolf at all. Then when a real wolf showed up, no one believed him.

It was going to take time. Time for him to show the community that he was a changed man. He had grown up in the eight years since he left Millers Creek. But since his return he had also matured in his faith. It took some time to get him there. But now that he had arrived, it would take time to show everyone this new truth of his. He couldn't expect anything more.

When he left the bishop's house the following week, he knew what lay before him. He could see the trials he had to endure. He knew what was at stake, and he was prepared. In his heart and in his mind, he was ready.

Martha squeezed his hand on the way home. "I'm proud of you," she said. She had ridden with him over to the bishop's house, but she had stayed outside in the buggy while he went in to talk to the man. And talk he did.

Samuel confessed all to the bishop. His time in prison, his *Englisch* wife, his *Englisch* baby and how their deaths came about. He told him of his promise to David that had led him right back there.

"Are you still going to fulfill that promise?" the bishop had asked. "If you truthfully want to marry Mattie Byler, I'll allow you to post that, but only after you show the sincerity of your heart."

Samuel shot him a sad smile. "No, I don't think that's going to be a possibility any longer. But I do want to come back and join the community. I know this is where I need to be. I'm ready to live the life I was born to live."

The bishop stood and offered his hand to Samuel. "That's just what I needed to hear."

"I just wish I hadn't messed things up with Mattie," he said to his sister.

Martha turned to look at him.

Samuel could feel her gaze on him, but he kept his firmly forward on the road ahead as he drove the buggy. He could always claim that driving on the main road through the valley required a lot of attention since there were so many cars and hills and places where bad accidents could happen. He could use that as his excuse for not looking at his sister. But the truth was, if he met her gaze, he wasn't sure he could keep himself together.

"You love her," she said in awe.

Samuel swallowed hard, then gave a quick nod. *"Jah."* He had never thought it possible. He never even dreamed that he would find love again nor had he ever imagined that he would fall in love with his brother's widow. He supposed that in itself was proof that God had a plan. Something he had begun to accept more and more in the days since Christmas. "I do."

"Does she return your feelings?"

Samuel bit back a sigh. "She did, and then she found out about Emma and Sadie before I had a chance to tell her and—" He shook his head. "I messed up."

"Surely not so much that she can't forgive you."

"I know she'll forgive me," he said with confidence. "But I so badly bruised everything she felt for me by not telling her the truth, and then having her find out from Eleanor Peachey."

Martha whistled under her breath. *"Jah,"* she said. "That's gotta be rough."

"I just hope maybe someday she and I can be friends. I enjoy working on her farm. And her daughters are precious and—"

"She's family," Martha said.

"Jah," he returned. She was family, and she would always be family. Yet just because you were family didn't mean you were friends. The saddest part of all was he wanted to be more than friends.

"Hmm," Martha mused. "Maybe after your shunning is all done and over with, we should have a family dinner."

Samuel shook his head. "No, Martha. Let it go. Mattie is a kind and good person. I did her wrong. Let her have her peace now."

"I've never known you to give up so easily," Martha said. She pressed her lips together in a disapproving frown.

"I told you," he said. "I'm a brand-new man."

One day flowed into the next. For Mattie, it was harder to go through David's things than she had thought it would be. Harder than she had ever imagined. Somehow, she managed.

She gathered up all the little pieces of his life: his clothes, pants and shirts, and started dispersing them to people she knew would need such things. She left his muck boots in the barn, but for the most part cleaned out the trivial pieces of his life. The important things she kept for his daughters, and the child she still carried. For the children she had his Bible, the wedding sampler that Evie had made when she and David had married and the book he'd written all his notes and thoughts in. It was a miscellaneous journal filled with whatnots. Sometimes it was a Bible verse, sometimes information on the goats, notes on cheese making, ideas for the store. Just a jumble of the offerings in David's brain. These things she saved for the kids. One day she would give them each one piece. When they were older and could appreciate the sentimental value.

Still, she couldn't help thinking about Samuel and the promise he said he had made to David. In the weeks since she had started clearing through David's things, she had read every word of that journal. There was not one mention of a promise. It made her sad to think that it wasn't true. Why she needed that promise as a comfort she didn't know. She wouldn't marry Samuel now. There was too much standing between them. He was just now getting himself right with the church. And he rarely spoke to her, if at all, when they met at the services. It'd been a month already since he had bent the knee before the congregation and confessed his sins, his life outside of Millers Creek. She had cried when he told of his wife and child and the heartache that he had suffered at their deaths. How he had turned away from God instead of toward Him. How he now wanted to make that right. He told of his confession to the court, of the crimes he was punished for, and his time in prison. She wasn't the only one with tears in her eyes that day. Of course the church voted that he be allowed to return. After an eight week shunning in which he was to reflect and pray on the sins he had committed and the change that was to come, he would be welcomed back. Four more weeks and he would be free of his *Bann*.

Before then, she would have this baby. She would pick out a name; she would nurse it, and bathe it, and feed it, alone.

The one other thing of David's that she wanted to keep was his baseball glove, but she hadn't been able to find it anywhere. As the girls napped and she did the dishes, she thought about the one place it might be.

She wiped her hands on a dish towel and made her way through the living room into the hall closet. Both her sisters were gone. Naomi was at their *dat*'s cleaning the *dawdihaus*, and Evie was with Helen Schrock. Shock of shocks, Helen had broken off her engagement with Freeman Yoder.

It was the scandal that rocked Millers Creek and pushed Samuel's transgressions down on the list of most talked about these days.

Mattie didn't know what happened between the couple, and she hadn't had a chance to press Evie for any details. Her sister left early and came home late. Sometimes didn't come home at all. But soon maybe she would know what had happened between the pair. Like it was any of her business. But with the way her life was going these days... She needed all the excitement she could get, even if it was someone else's excitement.

She opened the door to the hall closet and peered up to the top shelf. There it was. David's baseball glove. Right next to his winter hat.

She slowly took the hat down from the shelf and closed the door. She didn't need the baseball glove. She just needed to know where it was. But his hat. She remembered vaguely moving it to the hall closet at some point in the winter. Just to get it away from all the hooks. When it had only been the two of them, there were plenty of hooks for their capes and coats and hats and scarves, but with her two sisters staying there, if anybody else came, there wasn't enough room. So the hat went into the hall closet. There it had stayed until now.

She lifted the hat to her nose and inhaled. It still smelled like him, like David and sweat and maybe a touch of goat. But the scent made her smile. She opened her eyes and looked down to the hatband. There was a piece of paper sticking out from around the inside edge.

What was that?

Somehow, just somehow, she knew that piece of paper was important. With trembling fingers, she reached in and plucked it out.

She started to read, slowly, then eyes still on the paper, she made her way over to the table and eased down into one of the chairs. Her legs were trembling more than her fingers, and tears filled her eyes as she read.

All anyone could talk about in Millers Creek was the breakup of Helen Schrock and Freeman Yoder. Even after Mattie had the baby, another girl, congratulations went around and the attention swung back to the young couple.

But when rumor came around that Samuel was leaving Millers Creek, Mattie didn't know whether to laugh, cry or scoff at the news. How could he be leaving Millers Creek? He had only so recently come back home. And after reading that letter that David had left in his hat, right under her nose and yet so far out of reach, the thought of Samuel leaving broke her heart all over again.

Davida, named after her father of course, was three weeks old when Evie came home early from Helen's.

"I don't know what's gotten into her," Evie said as she ate a piece of Naomi's latest creation, a peppermint chocolate cheesecake.

Frankly, after giving birth and all the hormone changes around the holidays, the recipe sounded nauseating to Mattie. But it seemed as if Evie was enjoying it.

Mattie was just enjoying holding her new baby while her older daughters sat at the table and happily colored in their coloring books.

"What did she say again?" Mattie asked. It seemed as if every night when Evie came home, she had a different reason why Helen called off the engagement of what was to be the wedding of the community. Helen and Freeman had been a couple for as long as the three of them—Helen, Freeman and Evie—had been friends. First grade.

"She says she's restless. That she's been too secluded here in this valley. She wants to go to Lancaster."

"And live with the *Englisch*?" Mattie asked, then she pressed a kiss to the top of her sweet baby's head. She really was a precious baby girl, her last gift from David.

"I don't know. I don't think so. She's been saying something about some distant cousin or whatnot there. That she could go and live and experience, I don't know, I guess a faster life."

They were all considered Old Order Amish, the yellow toppers, black toppers and white toppers there in the valley, and the Lancaster Amish who drove the gray buggies. But in Lancaster life was much more commercial. There were lots of tourists and lots of tourist attractions owned and run by Amish. Some were owned and run by *Englisch* who pretended to be Amish. But it was definitely more bustling than quiet Kishacoquillas Valley.

"And she thinks she's going to be happy there?"

"I suppose," Evie said, scraping up the last bite of cheesecake and licking it off her fork. "The thing I don't get is she didn't even ask Freeman if he would move there after they got married."

"Have you talked to him?"

"I tried, but he considers me in Camp Helen. So he's not saying much. I know he's heartbroken. How could he not be?"

And Evie was heartbroken for him. Mattie so wanted to tell her sister that this might be her opportunity to show Freeman there were other fish in the sea besides Helen Schrock. But Evie just wasn't that kind to step in and take advantage of the situation that was hurting the other people involved.

Mattie considered her noble. But this was Evie's happiness at stake as well. Though every time Mattie mentioned it, Evie aggressively denied that she had any feelings other than friendship for Freeman. Half of Millers Creek knew that to be an understatement. But having gone through falling in love and then losing that love… If she could do it over again, she would. Even though it was the hardest thing she had ever done.

A knock sounded at the door. Evie grabbed one crutch and her plate. She stood. "I'll get it."

"Danki," Mattie said.

Evie made her way over to the table and set her saucer there before grasping the door handle and opening it.

"Samuel," she gasped.

Mattie looked up just as Evie's head swiveled in her direction.

Samuel?

"Hi, Evie. Can I come in?"

Samuel. She would have known that voice anywhere. It was strong and true though she never realized it before, and it seemed threaded with steadfastness and security. Though somehow in all the times that she talked to him since his return, she had never noticed how the mere sound of his voice made her feel safe. Not until now. When it was too late.

"Jah, jah." Evie stepped back to allow him room to enter. "Come in."

Mattie's breath caught in her throat as he stepped inside and took off his hat. He twirled it around on his fingers as Evie shut the door behind him.

"Samul," Bethann squealed and hopped down from the table. She ran over to give him a big hug, practically plastering herself to his legs.

From her place in the high chair, Gracie patted her hands against the tray, chanting, "Me, me, me."

He bent down and scooped Bethann into his arms.

Tears filled Mattie's eyes. To see him holding her daughter brought back memories of David, but yet not. Seeing Samuel hold Bethann again brought forth all the possibilities that seemed to haunt her.

"I better get Gracie out before she tears apart that tray." Evie laughed.

Samuel stood there, still holding Bethann but not saying a word as he waited for Evie to free the toddler. Once she was down and had clumsily made her way over to where he stood, he scooped her up on the other side.

It was almost more than Mattie could take.

He turned to her and cleared his throat. "I really came to talk to you about something."

"Okay." What else could she say?

He lowered the girls to the floor, and Evie reached out a hand to Bethann. "Get your sister," she said. "We'll go upstairs and work on puzzles. How does that sound?"

"No," Bethann said. "Gracie eat them."

"Well," Evie said. "We'll just get Gracie one to eat and us one to put together."

Evie was trying so hard to give her and Samuel a moment alone. Like it mattered. That moment of whatever it was between them had come and gone. She might still love him with all her heart. She probably always would. Yet he didn't seem to feel the same. Still, she had loved and lost David. She had recovered, and she would recover from this as well.

"Okay," Bethann said, but she didn't seem very happy about it.

Samuel waved to the girls as they headed up the stairs. Once they disappeared into their room, he came all the way into the living room and sat, or rather perched, on the edge of her sofa.

"Davida?"

"It seemed appropriate," Mattie said.

Samuel nodded. "It's perfect."

"Do you want to hold her?" she asked. If he had been any other male from their church congregation she wouldn't have even dreamed to ask if he wanted to hold a barely three-week-old baby, but Samuel was different. He was her baby's uncle, a man who might have once been her daddy.

Samuel swallowed hard and shook his head. "No," he said, though the one word was barely a whisper. He clasped his hands together between his knees. "I came to tell you that I'm leaving Millers Creek."

So the rumors were true.

"Why?" He'd just gotten everything back right with the church. He had just finished his shunning. He was back in the fold. Why was he going now? "You're not going back to live with the *Englisch* are you?" The thought made her stomach ache. He had come so far, endured so much, more than any one man probably ought to have to endure in a lifetime. He needed to stay close, home, where they could look after each other and care for one another as family should. Because whether they had a romantic relationship or not, they were still family. And they had an obligation to each other.

He chuckled ruefully. "No, I'm not going to go back in with the *Englisch*. But I thought I might go back out to New Wilmington. See what the church has to offer for me out there."

Mattie shook her head, trying so hard to understand. "Why would you go out there to see what the church has to offer you when the church here has so much for you?"

"It's harder being home than I thought."

Mattie stared at him for a moment. "Hard? What are you talking about?"

"Just hard." He stood then. "I wanted to tell you myself."

She was on her feet in a heartbeat, the motion disturbing Davida just a bit. The baby whimpered, then balled one hand into a fist and stretched. "So that's it then?" An uncharacteristic anger rose within her. "You're just gonna walk away from the promise you made your brother?"

He turned and started for the door but stopped and swiveled back to face her. "Last I heard, you didn't even believe we made promises."

"Last you heard was wrong," she said quietly, confidently. "I found a letter that David left. I was cleaning through his things. It told me about your promise. And now you're just gonna walk away from it because it's hard."

Samuel stopped. She could almost see him processing the words, trying to figure out exactly what she meant by each of them.

Mattie kept her gaze firm and strong on his, as she waited for him to grasp her meaning.

"That promise was to marry you."

"Actually, it was to take care of us. All of us. Me, Bethann, Gracie and Davida. Even though she wasn't even born when you guys made that promise. That's still what he meant. And now you're telling me that you can't do that."

"I'm telling you that I can't live in the same church district with you and be in love with you and not be able to come home to you every night."

"So you do want to marry me." The bold words slipped from her as easy as silk.

"At first it was to fulfill the promise," he said. "I explained all this to you. But then as I got to know you better, I fell in love with you. And then I messed it all up. I can't stay here and not be married to you. But if I hadn't wanted to be married to you, I wouldn't have asked you to start with."

Mattie cradled the sleeping baby in her arms and carried her toward the small bassinet they had set up in the living room. She placed her daughter there with minimal fuss then turned around to face this stubborn man.

"I don't recall you asking to marry me at all. Not even once."

"Of course I did—I came and said—"

"You came and said 'I'm going to marry you.' That's not asking."

"Like it makes a difference." He said the words, but she could see the hope flare in his eyes.

"Maybe you should give it a try," she boldly said.

He swallowed hard and walked slowly to where she was standing in the middle of the living room. He was barely aware of Evie at the top of the staircase, watching everything, and he wondered if Naomi was lurking around the side of the kitchen door.

That didn't matter now. All that mattered was him and Mattie and the promise he'd made to his brother and the love that he'd found so unexpectedly.

He took her hands into his and stared into those eyes so green. "Mattie Byler, will you marry me?"

"Samuel Byler, I thought you'd never ask."

* * * * *